Living It Up

Ann Jennings

Maximize Publishing Inc.

2018 Monterey Ave

Bronx N.Y. 10457

Attn.: Michael McCain

C/o: Kevin Brown

Kelby Lott

ISBN-13: 978-0692301623
ISBN-10: 0692301623

Maximize Publishing Inc.

(Retail Price 21.99)

Living It Up- Ann Jennings

Living It Up

Ann Jennings

Living It Up- Ann Jennings

Living It Up- Ann Jennings

When the school bus picked seventeen year old Tori Spellman up for school that morning at six thirty, she knew it wasn't going to be a good day. The feeling she was having when she woke kept telling her to stay home. When the bus pulled into the high school she couldn't hold it any longer. Now everyone is going to know Tori thought. Why did I have to get sick on the bus? The boys were concerned, but she heard the whispers from the girl's and knew that they knew. It was no way to fool them. Even though Tori still wore her same cloths and kept her hourglass figure she knew it would not be long before she wouldn't be able to get into her fashionable cloth's that she loved so much.

When the bus driver stopped in front of the high school she asked Tori if she needed a nurse. Even though Tori liked the nurse at their school she wasn't ready for anyone to know yet. Tori said no, trying to be strong with her head down and her knees weak hoping she wouldn't faint. Tori let everyone get off the bus first disobeying the rules that Ms. Jo had set at the beginning of school year teaching the boys be gentleman and get off last. She was pretending to get all her books together, fasten her jacket and put on lip gloss, being careful not to make eye contact with Ms. Jo the driver.

With her head still down Tori walked to the front of the bus and told Ms. Jo that she had gotten most of it up. "No problem" Ms. Jo told her, I'll take care of it. Ms. Jo was the best driver Tori had out of all the twelve years she's been riding the Cook County Public School bus. Letting kid's sit where they wanted and helping you with homework questions on the way to school when you didn't understand.

One very cold morning they arrived at school five minutes early, Ms. Jo pulled out doughnuts and hot chocolate in a thermos, then passed out paper cups to everyone. All the kid's on Tori's bus also agreed that she was the best bus driver they ever had. She made the boys be gentlemen's and let the girls off the bus first, and then they would get up and exit the bus, none of the boys mind doing this and their parents thought this was a good thing she was doing. Tori got off the bus without looking at her. As she walked into the school she wondered if Ms. Jo had figured out her secrete but like Ms. Jo she didn't say anything.

Living It Up- Ann Jennings

Tori thought she was waiting for her to speak up first. Tori was just hoping to finish this last year of school wishing it was May, but it was only October the second month of school. Dominique kept asking Tori when she was going to tell her mom and stepdad but Tori kept telling him the same story, "when the time is right" actually she wanted to wait till she started showing just to give herself more time. The truth was she wasn't scared of what her mom would say but how her stepdad would feel, she was his little girl, he married Tori's mom when she was only three and her brother Ronald was five.

Tori's mom told her that he took them from rags to riches. They had the biggest house on the block with a guest house in back that's bigger than everyone else regular house. Her stepdad Eugene owned Capable Hands Insurance Company which employees about two hundred. The Company belonged to his grandfather then his dad now it was his. Eugene has a son from his first marriage Kenny who was older than them and doesn't want any part of the insurance company. Kenny says "all the people there are all stuck up with their three piece suits and fifty dollar ties." He said he'd rather work with his hands and be comfortable.

Eugene asked Ronald if he would like to come to work with him after he graduated from college but Ronald said no he wanted to go to Harvard and studying Psychology saying he wants to get into people's head. So that leaves Tori. She didn't want to run it either but she would do it because she didn't want to hurt her stepdad's feelings. Her mom Cindy said all Tori had to do was give him one of them prize winning smiles and he would do anything for her. Tori never got to meet her real dad he died when she was only three years old. Cindy met Ronald the kid's dad when she was in college, he was in her trigonometry class.

Cindy would always ask questions on things she didn't understand. So one day, Ronald told her to come to the tutoring class on Saturday morning in the computer center and they could help her with all her questions. Cindy thanked him and that next Saturday she showed up at the college and he was there. Cindy sat next to him with her book and he smiled at her. You can ask them anything you want here and they will answer all your questions and go over it with you until you get it, I love coming here.

For the next three years Cindy took his advice and they would meet for tutoring on Saturday mornings then go to lunch before they went home. During the summer months they would work to help their parents out with college tuition. They even took some of the same classes to share books to save their parents money, then in Cindy's third year she found out she was pregnant, they got married and Cindy dropped out but Ronald stayed to finish. Ronald Jr. was born and they were such a happy little family. Cindy told her mom one day she would go back to school and finish college but she found herself always busy with the baby.

Ronald Jr. wanted all her attention; she had to hold him while she cooked and when she vacuumed. She couldn't take showers she could only take a bath if he was sitting in his baby chair next to the tub watching her or she would wait until Ronald came home and take a shower. When Ronald Jr. turned two Cindy found out she was pregnant again Ronald was thrilled and he took his wife and Ronald Jr. out for dinner to celebrate. I hope it's a girl this time her husband said "no" I want a brother Ronald Jr. said standing in the chair, everyone in the restaurant heard him and laughed.

Nine months later Tori was born and Ronald fell in love with his little sister always wanting to hold her and feed her. Ronald got a job with a major construction company with his brilliant math skills they had him drawing up blue prints, you just tell him what you want and Ronald could draw it up. The company was given a thirteen million dollar contract to build an entire subdivision which would have forty five homes. On the third home Ronald was called over to straighten out some confusion with measurements on the stairs, according to his blue print drawing there were to be fourteen stairs but when the builder's started to build the stairs they could only fit thirteen. Ronald was called to the sight and went up on the second level to show them how the top step would curve in a two degree angle to make the fourteenth stair Ronald took a wrong turn falling to the lower landing having a heart attack on his way down.

Cindy kept a picture of him on her night stand in her room next to the bed. Tori had his eyes and Ronald had his smile. He was a handsome man and from the picture Tori saw that he was tall and towered over her mom even with her hills on. Cindy would always catch Tori in her room looking at the picture that's when she started telling her that's daddy and Tori would kiss the picture and say hi daddy. Ronald never looked at the picture he was mad at his dad for dying and leaving them. But only being five he was too young to understand.

Cindy didn't take them to their father's funeral because she wanted them to always remember him like the last time they saw him. Then when Eugene came into their lives Ronald wasn't angry any more he instantly fell in love with Eugene and Eugene fell in love with them. He had Kenny every weekend and every summer, then when he married Cindy all three kids got alone great. Tori wanted all Eugene's time from the time he came home from the insurance company Tori stuck by his side. She was the first to call him daddy then Ronald finally came around. Tori didn't want her mom to tuck her in at night any more she always wanted Eugene to read her a good night story every night and stay until she fell asleep then the first thing the next morning she would wake to say good bye to him before he went to the office.

On weekends she would want him to play dolls with her or take her to the park or play tea party with her with her little toy dishes. Cindy would make little snacks for her and Eugene and put them on her little plates and put tea in her little teapot. Tori would pour tea from the pot into a little tea cup and offer it to her dad, and Eugene would say you make the best tea and this would give Tori a laugh. When Tori started school Eugene would drop her off on his way to the Insurance Company every morning then in third grade Tori met Leigh Kay and wanted to ride the bus with her. She still loved her dad but always wanted to be with Leigh Kay and Eugene saw how happy his little girl was with her new friend and was happy to share her.

When Leigh Kay came to spend the night Tori told her father he didn't have to read her a story but the next night when Leigh Kay wasn't there Tori wanted to hear her good night story. After a stormy night Cindy and Eugene would always find Tori curled up asleep at the foot of their bed. When Cindy would go out of town on business trips with Eugene for Capable Hands Tori would insist on going with them leaving Ronald and Kenny with friends. It was hard to separate the two. Tori would do anything for her dad and Eugene would do anything for his daughter.

In third grade Tori had seen pregnant women before and had always wondered how their skin could stretch like that. I couldn't do it she told Leigh Kay when I get married and get pregnant I'm not leaving the house I've seen them maternity clothes and they're not very attractive. Leigh Kay laughed and told her they're going to have to come up with some name brand maternity clothes for you and they have to match Tori said. I can't imagine you without matching clothes and in a big ugly dress Leigh Kay said and both girls laughed, in grammar school Tori would not leave the house without her clothes, shoes and hair done. All her cloths had to match and they had to be name brand, Tori said she wouldn't be caught dead in an off brand name right down to her underwear, her bra and panties had to be a matched set and if she wore a slip it had to match her underwear.

Cindy didn't know why her daughter was like this Tori would cry if she made her wear shoes that didn't match her outfit or under ware that didn't match or jeans that was last year's design. Running late for school one morning Tori couldn't find her red bra to match the red panties she had on and cried when Cindy made her ware the pink bra because they were running late. Tori got sick at school and the nurse called Cindy to come pick her up. Since that incident Cindy would not let her daughter wear anything that didn't match or out of style. She's just all girl Eugene would say I think it's cute. You don't think she has a problem Cindy asked concern, no she love to be a girl Eugene said thinking of an excuse for his daughter she just love to be a girl and most girls like her won't give their parents any trouble because they think it may spoil their image "What?" Cindy said confused and they both laughed.

Eugene liked Dominique but Tori didn't know how he would feel about him after she tells him their news. Eugene had always wanted a daughter. After Kenny was born his ex-wife said "That's it" giving birth was the worse pain she had ever experienced and she swore never to do it again. This made Eugene very sad knowing his son would never have a little sister or brother to play with or share his toys or his deepest secrets with. Raising just Kenny the house was always quiet no kids running around chasing each other, playing tag or hide and go seek, no tattle tailing, no Saturday afternoon board games at the kitchen table.

This is the way Eugene was raised and he had always said he would never have just one child ever since Eugene could remember he had asked his mom and dad for a little brother or sister he remembered walking to school alone every morning after his dad left to buy fresh Danishes on his way to work and walking home every afternoon for lunch which he ate alone at the kitchen table while his mom did her chores around the house and his dad was at Capable Hands Insurance company working. After lunch he would walk back to school alone and back home again alone at three.

Eugene had friends but all his friends had brothers or sisters or both. In sixth grade Eugene would spend the night with friends and have fun playing with them and their siblings then the next morning he would hate when his mom came to take him home. That would be one of the times he would ask for a brother but the answer was always no. But he would keep asking hoping one day they may change their minds. His parents would always see Eugene's expression change from the time they picked him up at his friends and when they got him home. When they got him home Eugene would go up to his room and play with his toy all alone playing with his little Indian and cowboy toys talking in his own voice for the Indian then turning to the cowboy toy man and talking in another voice.

When his mom would call him down for dinner he would sit at the table with his parents and listen to them talk back and forth about adult things nothing Eugene would be interested in and most of the time they was talking he didn't know what they were talking about and when he would ask they would only say adult stuff. When Eugene started high school he had lots of friends but he still wanted a brother or sister and that's when he finally gave up asking. He told himself when he get married he would have a house full of kid's.

In his senior year he already knew he wasn't going to college because he had to go work with his dad at Capable Hands just like his dad had to do when he graduated from high school some of his friends were jealous of him saying after he graduate he already had a job waiting for him. On Christmas morning his parents would watch him open all his presents but he had no one to compare his toys with he couldn't say "look what mine can do" or "why did he get more toys then me." It just never happened, his parents were in their thirty's now and he thought too old to have more kids.

His dad had one brother but their ages were so far apart they never got to be best friends his uncle was born when his grandparents first got married and after many years they thought they couldn't have any more kid's Eugene's dad was born when his uncle was in high school. Eugene's mom told him he would be ok she didn't have any brothers or sisters and she didn't complain. Dominique and Tori were voted best looking couple for the year book in their junior year last year and everyone said they would get it again this year. They said there's no girl that comes close to Tori's looks or any boy that comes close to Dominique's looks.

Everyone was envy of the couple and wanted to hang around them and be their friend. Dominique had the type of body you would see in a workout magazine and his body could get him a job as a model or even in playboy. The girls always smiled when he walked by them in the hall between class but they knew him and Tori would be together forever, but one couldn't help but melt when they saw him. Tori had the same effect on the boys with her hourglass figure she knew she looked good and knew that the boys liked looking at her, so she would strut around in her short skirt or ware tight shorts just enough to tease them.

They waited until she walked by and whistled and she loved the attention and thought all the boys were cute. This went on until late October before Thomas Middleton transferred to their school. All the girls went crazy over him, Tori's best friend Leigh Kay said she had to have him. While all the girls were drooling over Thomas Tori kelp her cool knowing she had the next best looking boy at school. All the boys at school didn't make friends with Thomas because they didn't want their girlfriend's to leave them for him.

Now it was Thomas who turned all the girls heads even Tori's. He had that smooth chocolate skin and killer smile with teeth as white as snow he was also tall like Dominique but not as muscular. Both boys had the same schedule and quickly became best friends you didn't see one without the other. When they walked down the hall the girl's would just stand aside and look.

On November third Tori stayed after school to watch Leigh Kay at cheer leader practice. After practice they walked to the drugs store for an ice-cream bar, that's when Tori told her friend her news. I was wondering when you were going to tell me Leigh Kay said as they walked eating their ice cream I thought I was your best friend. You are Tori said, well why am I the last to know? Tori shouted you're not the last to know you're the third. Dominique and I haven't told anyone yet, not even our parents. I knew something was wrong when you started to get dizzy all the time Leigh Kay shot back at her friend. I was having headaches Tori said. "Yea right" Leigh Kay said I'm mad at you right now, I don't like when you keep secretes from me.

The light was changing yellow when Leigh Kay ran across the street and Tori followed trying to explain to her friend why she didn't tell her right away but the car turning the corner couldn't stop fast enough to keep from hitting her. Leigh Kay ran back to her friend lying in the street screaming her name" Tori Tori" wake up someone please help us Leigh Kay cried out.

The Chicago Police and an ambulance were called and everyone checked out ok except Tori. Leigh Kay told the police that Tori was four months pregnant so they went to inform the paramedics. She was taken to Mercy Hospital in the ambulance with Leigh Kay right by her side.

Living It Up- Ann Jennings

On the way she called Dominique then Tori's parents. After Tori was checked by the Dr. and released she walked into the waiting room to see her mom, Leigh Kay, Dominique and Thomas talking quietly in the corner and her stepfather pacing the floor biting his nails. He was the first to see her and ran to her and gave her a big hug. Tori honey you scared me, are you ok? Every one fussed over her until her dad said let's take her home. All four kids' got into the back seat of Eugene's Cadillac and Cindy sat in the front. When they got back to Tori's house they all sat around in the dining room and the truth came out. Dominique spoke up first and said we're getting married.

Eugene Spellman stood and said "No you're not" I think you have done enough damage around here. I want to see a diploma before I see a marriage license. Tori's mom was hurt she said she hadn't felt such hurt since Tori and Ronald's dad died. After Dominique finish talking to Tori's parents Eugene told Dominique to leave. I think you should go home and talk to your parents. Leigh Kay called her mom to tell her she was spending the night which wasn't unusual for her.

Tori and Leigh Kay talked long into the night. Tori told her she was upset with her for telling the police her secret but was glad everything turned out ok. You're upset with me Leigh Kay shot back that car could have killed you. What was I supposed to do? I was upset with you for holding back on me. I'm sorry Tori said I just wanted to hold to my secret a little longer. It's a good thing that car wasn't't speeding Leigh Kay said or we wouldn't be having this conversation right now. I know Tori said I'm sorry I screamed at you, no I screamed at you first Leigh Kay said and I should never have ran and left you like that.

Did it hurt much when it hit you Leigh Kay asked? No I think the sound of the tires scared me more than anything but it did hurt when I hit the ground, you think the baby's ok Leigh Kay asked concern. They checked the baby on the sonogram and the doctor says he looks fine. I'm glad you're ok Leigh Kay said I don't know what I'll do without you, well I won't give you a chance Tori said because I'm going to be around a long time. When I saw you lying there in the street I almost lost it I have never been so scared in my life. Good night Tori, good night Leigh Kay.

Living It Up- Ann Jennings

By March Tori was eight months alone and had only gained fifteen pounds and still looked great. Mrs. Spellman had to buy her prom dress two sizes larger to accommodate her budge in the middle. She told her mom and Leigh Kay maybe she shouldn't go to the prom this year but they had to talk her into it saying this would be the last prom she would ever go to plus her and Dominique had won king and queen last year at their junior prom and more than likely they would win again this year for senior prom.

Tori told them now she knew how the turkey felt on Thanks giving when her mom stuffed it with dressing, all the girls laughed. Leigh Kay's mom was a seamstress and made her dress every year. Leigh Kay's dress was long and light pink and Tori's was short and hot pink. The next day both girls took the bus to the mall to buy shoes to go with their dress. Tori usually wore very high hills but this time she thought she should wear flats.

Living It Up- Ann Jennings

Leigh Kay noticed the look on her friends face and held up a pair of flats and said these are so cute I think I'll buy these to go with my dress. Next they went to Clair's and bought earrings, their last stop was Burger King to get something to eat before taking the bus back home. When they walked into Burger King Tori spotted her step brother Kenny and his new girlfriend Barbara eating lunch. After the girls got their food they joined them at the table. So what's going on Kenny asked? Just shopping for the prom next Saturday Tori said. Oh the good old prom Kenny said rubbing his chin I remember those days, and then he got a kick from Barbara under the table. When they finished Barbara offered to give them a ride home.

Living It Up- Ann Jennings

When they got home they showed Tori's mom everything they had bought and Tori gave her mom's credit card back to her. Kenny and his girlfriend went into the din to say hi to Eugene. I thought you had classes today his dad said I did Kenny said Biology. Tori and Leigh Kay went up to her room to listen to music; they turned the music up and danced to their favorite cd. After two hours Leigh Kay came down to go home Kenny and Barbara was on their way out and offered her a ride home.

You girls did a good job today Cindy told them again the shoes and the earrings are a perfect complement to the dress. What about my hair Tori said? You can go next weekend and get it done her mom said, and my nails too Tori asked? Sure Cindy said I can't let the queen go around with her nails not done they all laughed.

Living It Up- Ann Jennings

The next Saturday on the morning of the prom Tori's mom dropped her and Leigh Kay off at the mall to get their hair and nails done and told them to call when they were finished and she would pick them up. Unless we run into Kenny and Barbara Tori said laughing. When they entered the mall Thomas and his mom Sheeree was on their way out, Thomas introduced his mom to them saying he was there to buy new black dress shoes for tonight. The girls walked around the mall and decided to buy a soft pretzel and sit down and eat it before moving on. After they finished their pretzel they headed to the nail shop and got their nails and toe's done they paid the extra fifteen dollars and got the French tips.

After sitting in the shop to let their nails dry they headed to the Dominican shop to get their hair done where they saw allot of their class mates getting their hair done also. After waiting an hour when they got their hair set and got under the dryer they had to shout to hear each other. After they got their hair done they decided to get their makeup done and eyebrows arched. It was 2:30 when they finished and called Cindy to come pick them up. When they got into the car Cindy said you girls look very nice. What time will the limo get there Tori asked her mom? 7:30 Cindy said that gives you thirty minutes to get to the prom at eight.

Living It Up- Ann Jennings

Eugene had rented a hot pink limo the same color as Tori's dress. Cindy dropped Leigh Kay at home and Tori told her she would see her at the prom. That night Kenny and Barbara remembered Tori told them she was going to the prom so they came by to take pictures. Kenny gave her a kiss on the check and told her how pretty she looked. He was still taking pictures of the limo when it drove her away to pick up Dominique; as they drove the neighbor changed from all houses, manicured lawns, with sidewalks to apartment buildings and gas stations and run down corner stores.

When the limo stopped in front of Dominique's building he was standing outside with a big smile on his face and a corsage for Tori to wear on her wrist. Then when the limo pulled up to the prom everyone was looking to see who got out. The chauffeur got out and came around to open the door and Dominique got out all the girls clapped then when Tori got out all the boys whistled. They felt like movie stars as they walked into the prom. No one was on the floor so Tori grabbed Dominique's arm and dragged him to the floor. Should you be doing this Dominique asked? What about the baby? Its ok we're fine then everyone got up and joined them on the dance floor.

After three dances Tori asked Dominique to get her some punch. Leigh Kay and her date left the dance floor to sit with Tori you ok Leigh Kay asked? You look pale I'm fine Tori said. Dominique returned to the table with Tori's punch and the four of them sat and talked. Tori told Leigh Kay to go and enjoy herself she had, had enough dancing for the night. After one hour the food was served to the tables. Everyone was served ¼ of a chicken string bean, baked potato and toss salad. Then for desert warm brownies and vanilla ice cream was served.

 After dinner the year book committee got up to give the results of the votes, best looking male went to Dominique and best looking female went to Tori. Most likely to succeed went to Mattie Hunter. Then came the part everyone was waiting for king and queen. With almost 100% of the votes our king and queen for this year is Dominique Daniels and Tori Spellman. Everyone got to their feet and clapped for them; they were crowned and asked to take the first dance. The band started up again and they were on the floor again.

Living It Up- Ann Jennings

Leigh Kay told Dominique not to let Tori drink any of the punch because she just saw Andrew Douglas pour liquor in it. After the prom everyone was driving to the 51st street beach to make out. Tori told the limo driver that they were done with him and he could go home. They got in Leigh Kay's date car and went with them; when Tori got home at 1:00 a.m. she was glad she went and was on cloud nine and had the best time of her life. May third was graduation and Tori was unable to attend because she was in labor and the school told her that her diploma would be mailed to her.

Dominique, Thomas and Leigh Kay went out with some of the other seniors to party that night, Tori told them to have fun. The next morning Tori called to find out what she had missed but she couldn't get in touch with anyone. She tried back an hour later, still nothing. She tried all morning to contact Leigh Kay or Dominique. Then at twelve noon when Leigh Kay woke she called to check on Tori. That must have been some party last night Tori said. Leigh Kay told her they rented a suite at the Marriott and had a big party with about thirty seniors.

Living It Up- Ann Jennings

Leigh Kay and Tori had been friends since the third grade and she always knew when her friend was hiding something. So go ahead and tell me the bad news Tori said. Tori, Dominique had too much to drink and slept with three girls. After about two long silent minuets Leigh Kay said I'm sorry do you need for me to come over? Tori stood there holding the phone when water started pouring down her leg and she called out for her mom. Cindy Spellman raced into her daughters room and said let's go we're having a baby.

Eugene must have run every red light between their house and Mercy Hospital. Cindy sat in the back with Tori and called Dr. Eto and told him to meet them there, he told her to tell Tori to try not to push and for Cindy to time her pains. Forty five minutes after Tori arrived; Dominique Jr. showed his face into the world. Tori's mom said he was the most handsome baby she had ever seen. Leigh Kay came to the hospital and stayed all day with Tori but Dominique never showed. They couldn't reach him until two days later when Tori was released from the hospital to going home. He showed up to Tori's house with flowers and Tori told him it was over.

The next day Thomas came over to see the baby and told Tori to be patient with Dominique he just needed a little time. Tori told him to tell his friend she didn't ever want to see him again, and then she started to cry. Thomas rose from his chair and went to the couch where she was sitting and put his arms around her and told her things would be ok. "They both felt it at the same time." He looked at her and she looked at him and just like it was meant to happen they kissed.

Tori's mom came into the living room to get DJ to put him to bed. Tori and Thomas sat in the living room talking until 2 am. Tori told him Dominique's mom Gloria Daniels never approved of her or the baby and had never came to see him. When she does let's just hope she's sober Thomas said. Gloria Denials started drinking at the age of twelve and never stopped. She watched her mom have a drink with her breakfast then another one with her lunch then another one with dinner then another one before she went to bed. This was an everyday thing for Gloria then at age twelve she started to join her mother in having a drink with every meal and one before she could go to sleep.

Living It Up- Ann Jennings

She was able to hide it at school; no one suspected at least no one confronted her. After her freshman year in high school she decided she had, had enough school all she wanted to do now was stay home and drink with her mom. One day at the liquor store she met the most handsome man she had ever seen. He started drinking every day with her and her mom after dating for eight months she found out she was pregnant but when she told her boyfriend that was the last she talked to him, she was always hoping he would come back but he never did.

Her mom started using heavy drugs and three months later she was gone, Gloria was pregnant and all alone. Two weeks later Dominique came again to see his son while he held his son Tori noticed after seeing him all her old feelings for him were gone. She was surprised how they talked like sisters and brothers no more tingle in her body when she's with him no more twinkle in her eyes, all the feelings were gone when they talked Tori had no desire to jump into his arms and kiss him. He told Tori he asked her dad for a job at the Insurance Company but he said no. So he was working at the new gas station that just opened on the corner of his house.

One day I'm going to become manager he boasted, sticking his chest out Tori looked at him thinking what a loser. So you need anything he asked her? No Tori said my parents give us all we need. He played with his son for five minutes and told Tori if she needed anything she knew where to find him and then he left. Tori sat there playing with DJ until he fell asleep in her arms. She took him up and put him in his little bed that Eugene had bought for him next to her own. Cindy taped lightly on the door and entered Tori's room. He's sleeping like a champ Tori whispered.

Cindy walked toward the baby's bed and looked down at him. Thomas has been around a lot Tori's mom said he seems very polite, I like that young man. Tori's mom has never said that about Dominique. His mom Sheeree is pretty cool too Tori told her, I meet her before DJ was born and I would love for you two to meet one day.

So what are you saying Cindy asked? Are you seeing him now? What does Dominique have to say about it? I thought they were best friends. Slow down mom Tori said throwing her arms up, what's with all the questions? Besides he starts Florida State tomorrow and we won't be seeing each other. And as for Dominique it's over between us. This little man is the only thing we have in common now Tori said rubbing DJ's head while he slept.

Two weeks later Sheeree Middleton and her son drove down to Florida State University, the drive took them two days; they stopped in Tennessee and went to the aquarium a place they had always talked about visiting. This is beautiful Thomas told his mom sticking his nose to the aquarium glass mocking the fish inside. Look at the blue one over there his mom said pointing he's beautiful how do you know it's a boy Thomas said well I don't know his mom laughed as they moved to the next tank.

Wow is that a shark Thomas said? Yes it is his
mom said. They saw Nemo the clown fish,
amphibians, birds, invertebrates, mammals,
different plants in all different colors, reptiles
and butterflies. After they left the Tennessee
Aquarium and stopped for burgers they
checked into a hotel for the night before
continuing their journey. The next morning
they were up at five showered, dressed and
was on the road again at six thirty. Ill drive
Thomas said its ok you just relax his mom
said. Thomas leaned his seat back and put his
ear phones in his ears. After a few hours when
the sun came up Thomas took the ear phones
out and told his mom he was hungry.

Let's get gas first his mom said then we will
stop for breakfast she knew they were
somewhere in Georgia and had at least
another eight hours to go. At the gas station
Thomas pumped the gas while his mom went
inside. At the next pump a girl with a long
thick pony tail and freckles was putting gas
into her yellow mustang and said hello to him.
I see you're from Illinois Rosie Ann said, I'm
from Wisconsin. Thomas said my mom and I
are on our way to Florida State, it's a good
school Rosie Ann said on the way there myself,
are you alone Thomas asked looking into her
car where's your mom? She couldn't make it
she had to work.

When Sheeree came back to the car and they started back on their journey she asked Thomas who the girl was he was talking to. Her name is Rosie Ann Thomas he said and she's on her way to start Florida State also, was her parents in the car Sheeree said, no mom she's going alone, oh that poor girl Sheeree said they were too busy to see their little girl start college, she said her mom had to work Thomas said. But what if something happens to her car on the road Sheeree said, I hope everything works out for her Thomas said she seems really nice maybe I'll see her at school sometimes and offer her a ride home as far as Chicago and she can take the Mega bus from there to Wisconsin, Oh that would be nice Sheeree told her son.

There she is mom Thomas said pointing to the yellow mustang let's follow her to make sure she makes it there safe. With all the classes Thomas was taking at Florida State he still had time to talk to Tori and DJ every night. He told Tori he told Dominique about them and he told him it was cool. The following semester Thomas took less classes and was less stressed out but knowing most of it came from him being away from home and missing Tori. Leigh Kay wrote every week from Stanford. Tori looked forward to the letters keeping all of them in her top dresser drawer with a rubber band around them.

Living It Up- Ann Jennings

Leigh Kay knew Tori wanted to know everything she was doing at school so she gave her a weekly report of everything she did even what classes had the cutest boys. Thomas finished two years at Florida State then decided he didn't want to go to Florida State University any more. He didn't want to be that far away from Tori and DJ and his phone bill was getting expensive from the long daily phone calls. His mom took care of the arrangements and registered him in Illinois State University.

 DJ enjoyed his daycare while Tori worked at Capable Hands. The Capable Hands Insurance building was located in Hyde Park a very distinguished first-class up-scale neighborhood where all the mansions had maids and chauffeurs. The restaurants were top notch and always passed inspection with a one hundred. The building was built over seventy five years ago and still stood out with its three story mirror look and the walk way to the entrance was made of marble with light's and the lawns were always manicured with thousands of beautiful flower's.

Living It Up- Ann Jennings

The manicured bushes were the talk of the neighborhood they were shapes of all different animals they gave the building air of secession. Inside each office had glass door's letting you see in each one; the beautiful staircase lead up to Eugene's office, private bath and conference room. At the back of the building was the employee's lounge where the employees would go take their much needed break away from the phone's, a place where they could kick off their shoe's and enjoy a cup of hot coffee and a Danish which Eugene provided for them daily following his dad and granddad's ritual.

In the warmer months the employee's would go out back where there were benches put there by Eugene's dad with umbrella's to shield them from the Chicago sun. There were also bird baths and a pound and a beautiful flower garden with yellow carnation's, pink Lilly's, peach and red roses and always full of beautiful butterflies. The squalls and rabbit's would run around the garden as if playing tag. When the employee's took their break out there it was hard for them to go back inside. The grounds were accentuated by an array of lights. Inside each office had a large picture window, with a view that overlooked the beautiful Hyde Park, a desk witch held a computer and a phone with four lines.

Living It Up- Ann Jennings

The building was a big asset to the community the lights stayed on at night glowing and making the block bright displaying it's big clock on top and outside temperature. Everyone always depended on this information as they drove by. The all glass building was typical for the neighborhood probably worth a million dollars. Tori had her own office which came with lots of stares from the other employee's that had been with the company for years. But no one had the nerve to say anything to her. She was actually doing a better job than some of them, making the company lots of money with her fresh idea's convincing people to renew their policy when it was time to renew.

She would always bring up DJ saying just think about your kid's she would tell the policy holder you don't want to leave them without a soft cushion to fall back on, her soft voice did it every time. The policy holder liked the way she treated them on the phone explaining everything and answering all their questions. When one of the other agent's was having trouble getting a policy holder to renew they would transfer the call to Tori's office and she would get the job done.

Living It Up- Ann Jennings

While shoe shopping for DJ one day Tori started to get sick and had to run to the ladies' room dragging DJ behind her. Mommy slow down, you're going to fast, everyone in the shoe store was shearing at them. When she came out the shoe salesman told her she didn't look to good and she should go home, DJ got worried. In the car Tori started thinking back and didn't remember her last period. Mommy you forgot to stop for the red light, my teacher said we should always stop for the red DJ shouted at her. Then he went on to tell him yellow means wait and green means go. Tori was not listening to her son her mind was on more serious things.

Its ok DJ she finally assured him I'm fine thinking to herself I'll feel better after nine months. When Tori got home she sat DJ at the kitchen table with a sandwich and went upstairs to call Thomas. Are you sure he said? Well not 100% but pretty sure Tori told him. Thomas told her let's not panic yet until we know for sure. Can you make a doctor's appointment Thomas asked? Today is Saturday Tori snapped at him? Can you make one Monday from work Thomas asked? Keeping his voice calm because he knew she was upset. Yes I guess I can Tori said. Tori was glad the incident at the shoe store had escaped DJ's mind he didn't mention it to her parent's.

Living It Up- Ann Jennings

Ronald came by the next day for Sunday dinner which he had been doing for the last three weeks. From that Tori and her mom knew him and his girlfriend wasn't getting alone. Hey peanut he said to Tori a name he gave to her the first time he saw her when his parents brought her home. He told her he gave her that name because her head reminded him of a peanut. You don't look to well are you catching something? "No I'm fine", Tori reassured her brother then changed the subject before he elaborated on it.

Next Sunday maybe I'll cook and give mom a break she said thinking fast for something to say. Um... let me see I think I'm going to be sick next Sunday Ronald said giving everyone at the table a laugh. Tori took a deep breath because the tension was off her now. After dinner Ronald and Tori played a game of checkers which Eugene had taught them when they were young; Ronald always wins, but this time he let Tori win and she knew it. After they finished playing Tori told him that she had to go give DJ a bath.

Living It Up- Ann Jennings

Ok peanut Ronald said, but you take care of whatever you got. Tori jumped when her brother made that statement and looked in his eyes. You got it she told him then ran upstairs to run DJ's bath water in his tub. DJ was the only three years old in his day care that had his own bed room, play room and bath room. Their house had six bedrooms and five baths, a formal living room, dining room, din, office and an extra-large kitchen, with a family room in the down stairs finished basement. And behind that house was a guest house a smaller version of the main house four bedroom's three bath's a large kitchen and a large din.

They had a gardener that came every two weeks that kept the grounds manicured and planting beautiful flower's in winter and summer. That night after DJ went to sleep Tori sat up thinking about her brother; when Ronald was thirteen and graduating from the eighth grade before he left the school that Wednesday for the last time he said goodbye to all his friends and teachers. His favorite teacher Ms. Smith glasses always look like they were on upside down and she always seems to be chewing on something Ronald said he couldn't figure that out. She wrote in Ronald's book to always remember everything she taught him and he would go far.

Living It Up- Ann Jennings

Ronald and his best friend Henry had been friends through grammar and high school now they would be graduating and going on to the same college together. Well two more day's Ronald said as him and Henry walked home together on the last day of school carrying their cap and gown. Graduation was in two day's on Saturday at the Civic Center at two. When Ronald got home Cindy told him to try his gown on so she could see if it needed ironing. When he tried it on it brought a tear to her eyes. I'm so proud of you she told him and gave him a big hug Awe ma don't go getting tear's on my gown I have to turn it back in we only get to keep the tassel on the cap showing our school colors.

Then Ronald broke down, I'm scared the kids say collage is tough what if I'm not smart enough. Cindy hushed her son oh honey you'll be just fine, you're the smartest high school graduate I know. But you don't know any other graduates except Henry. Well you're smarter than him Cindy said now how about some milk and cookies Cindy said distracting him. That Saturday morning when Ronald came down Cindy had made a big breakfast for him with Tori's help. Still nerves Eugene asked him? Yes sir Ronald said sitting at the table, well just think in four years you'll be doing something you always wanted to do, study people and analyze the situation and you will have your own office and everyone will be calling you doctor.

"Not me" Tori said coming into the room good morning peanut Ronald said to his sister and I will properly be your first patient Eugene said. I can tell who fixed the toast Ronald said looking at his sister. It's not burnt Tori said just a little brown they all laughed then Kenny walked in and said I thought I smelled breakfast. Hey son Eugene said have a seat I'll get another plate Cindy said getting up "no sit" I got it Kenny said opening the cabinet to get a plate, no toast for me Kenny said and the laughter started all over again.

Are you wearing that his dad asked, no I have dress pants and shirt in the car Kenny said. After breakfast Cindy put the dishes in the dishwasher while everyone went up to get ready. They would all go to Ronald's graduation at two and then that evening at seven they would go to Kenny's graduation from the local college. Ronald said he wouldn't be able to make it to Kenny's graduation he would be hanging out with his friends. Eugene still couldn't get either son to take over the insurance business.

After Ronald's graduation Eugene gave him money and he left with his friends. When they got to the college at seven that evening Eugene let Cindy and Tori off at the front and went to park the Cadillac. They waited for him then they went in to find their assigned seat matching the number on their tickets. Tori sat between her parent's and Kenny's mother sat two seats away from them, Tori and Eugene was not on good terms. When Kenny was young every weekend Eugene would pick his son up and drop him off he would not get out the car he would just wait until he saw his son go inside the house before he drove off.

Living It Up- Ann Jennings

Kenny spotted them when the graduate's marched in and waved at them. When they called his name to walk across the stage Kenny got his diploma then threw his cap up in the air. After the graduation his mom wanted to take him to dinner but Kenny wanted to go with his friends so his mom just gave him money and kissed him good bye and asked him was he coming home that night? Don't wait up he told her. Then he went to say hi to his dad, Eugene slipped money into his sons hand and congratulated him. "Thank you dad", I'm going to hang out with friends tonight I'll stop by tomorrow.

The next day when Kenny and his girlfriend showed up at his dad's a new car was in the driveway with a big ribbon tied around it, I think you just got your first new wheels Brenda his girlfriend said. Kenny used his key to enter the house and called out "who got a new car?" you do his dad said," thanks' dad; Kenny said I love it the keys are in it Eugene said take it for a spin. Would you like a cup of coffee Cindy asked Brenda? While Eugene and Kenny went for a spin in Kenny's new car Brenda sat at the kitchen table drinking coffee and talking to Tori and Cindy they liked Brenda but they know it wouldn't last Kenny went through girlfriend's like DJ went through a box of his favorite cookies.

Living It Up- Ann Jennings

Kenny owned his own business. When Kenny opened Kenny's Style and Cut he had many customers all his friend's came every two weeks like clockwork, Shirley came every three weeks and Kenny liked her. She would bring her five year old son which she had in high school to Kenny's shop every third Saturday for a haircut. Shirley was the most beautiful girl Kenny had ever seen, her chocolate skin, her hair in twist, her nails and toes professionally done and her shape made Kenny melt.

She was the one that always brought him in and Kenny never saw a ring on her finger. She would always sit and read or talk on her cell phone while Kenny cut her son Kevin's hair then she would pay and leave. Kevin was the first to start a conversation with Kenny. Today's my birthday Kevin said jumping up in the barber chair one Saturday morning. How old are you Kenny asked? "No let me guess" 55? No Kevin said, 50? Kenny asked? No Kevin said, 45? Kenny said because you don't look a day over 45, are you married? No I'm only five Kevin said.

Kevin... his mom said from her chair, you don't have to tell everyone today's your birthday. Its ok Kenny said I like birthdays. How old are you Kevin asked Kenny. "Kevin" his mom said, no it's fine Kenny said I'm seven, you're seven? Kevin asked with a puzzled look on his face yes do I look older Kenny asked? Kevin just hunched his shoulders. All done Kenny said taking the cape off Kevin's shoulders. When Shirley went in her purse to try to pay Kenny told her "not today" it's free on kid's birthday and also you get this Kenny said handing Kevin a sucker.

Thank you Shirley said my name is Shirley I know Kenny said I'm Kenny and I own this place, it's a nice place you have here Shirley said, I love your hair Kenny told her, what does your husband think about it? I'm not married Shirley said, Kevin's dad and I broke up when I was still pregnant with him so it's just me and Kevin and we're not looking for anyone right now. Well how about dinner tonight to celebrate Kevin's birthday, with cake Kevin asked? Now what's a birthday dinner with no cake Kenny said. "Can we mom?" Kevin said.

Living It Up- Ann Jennings

Shirley started thinking, come on Kenny said it's not like I'm a stranger I have been cutting Kevin's hair for eight months now. I know Shirley said, ok I guess it will be ok; "Yea" Kenny and Kevin said and high fived each other. Can I pick you up Kenny said? No we will meet you at the restaurant Shirley said. What kind of car do you drive Kevin asked Kenny. I have an infinity Kenny said one year old I got it when I graduated from college last year "wow" that's a bad car Kevin said.

Here's my cell phone number Kenny said handing Shirley a piece of paper I close at eight but I can get someone to close for me Kenny said ok I'll call you Shirley said, bye little man Kenny said to Kevin and happy birthday. Kenny was all smiles after Shirley and Kevin left. At 1:00 when Glen the other barber came in that rented the other booth from Kenny he asked him if he would lock up for him tonight, is everything ok Glen asked?

Living It Up- Ann Jennings

Better than ok Kenny said; guess who has a date tonight? Both men gave each other high fives. Kenny left the shop in a good mood. He was living with his mom but still had his bed room at his dad's when his mom got on his nerves. This day he went to his moms because the outfit he wanted to wear was in his closet at his mom's house. His mom was surprised to see him. You're home early she said did you close early? No Kenny said I came home to change, I met a girl and I'm taking her and her five year old son out to dinner this evening.

Where's the father his mom asked, not in the picture Kenny said he left when she told him she was pregnant, just be careful his mom said. I will Kenny said running up the stairs, what's her name his mom called up the stairs but Kenny had already closed his bedroom door. Kenny showered and sat around waiting for Shirley to call him. When his cell phone rang he answered it on the first ring where should we meet you Shirley asked what do Kevin feel like eating Kenny asked I'll let you ask him Shirley said handing Kevin the phone. Hey birthday boy where would you like to go and eat? Subway Kevin said you're kidding right Kevin said, no I love Subway Kevin said I always get the B.L.T. on wheat. Ok let me talk to your mom Kenny said, when Shirley got back on the phone Kenny said is he serious?

Living It Up- Ann Jennings

He loves Subway's B.L.T. whenever I tell him we're going out to eat he always wants Subway. Ok Kenny said it's his birthday so Subway it is. I'm going to have to change clothes Kenny said. They made arrangements to meet at the Subway close to Shirley's house at five. Kenny changed his clothes and ran down the stairs and out the door, you're not wearing that are you his mom asked but Kenny had already closed the front door.

At Subway Kevin ordered his usual but this time he added a drink, chips and a cookie. Shirley ordered steak and cheese sub and Kenny ordered Teriyaki chicken. After they finished their sub they sang happy birthday to Kevin and share his cookie with them. How about tomorrow I bring over a real cake Kenny said, with ice cream Kevin said of course with ice cream Kenny said. I don't know Shirley said ok Kenny said why you don't and Kevin come to my house tomorrow and I will have my mom make us a cake, ok Shirley said.

Kenny wrote his address on a napkin and told her to come over about three. Kenny said goodbye to them and they all went home. The next morning Kenny asked his mom about the cake and she wrote him a list and sent him to the store for ingredients. At three Shirley and Kevin showed up and Kevin saw presents on the table. Are these for me "Kevin" Shirley said its ok Kenny said they're for him, can I open them Kevin said. Let me introduce you to my mom first Kenny said. He took them to the kitchen where his mom was just putting a cherry on top of the cake. "Wow" is that mine Kevin said? It sure is Kenny's mom said Kenny's mom fell in love with Shirley and he son.

After their little party Kenny took them to meet his dad. Eugene, Cindy and Tori fell in love with them also. After dating for eight months Kenny moved in with Shirley and Kevin. They loved having him around and after a year Shirley quit her job and joined Kenny in his. Ronald was graduating from Harvard with a degree in psychology Cindy was so proud of him. Eugene purchased their plane tickets and rental car on line, three two way tickets and one way tickets because Ronald would be coming back home with them. They flew in a day before the graduation Ronald had to go for graduation practice at the civic center Cindy told him to take their rental car they wouldn't be using it.

On the way Ronald stopped and picked up a few of his friends. Tori told her mom she saw a cute dress in one of the little boutique shops in the lobby so they went down to the lobby and inside the store Tori tried on the little hot pink dress with the back poker dot collar Cindy told her it looked nice on her. Cindy bought herself a new dress also. On the way out Tori spotted a little pink purse with a black strap in the same color as her dress. Cindy spotted it also and told her to go get it. Thanks mom Tori said placing a wet kiss on her mom's cheek and ran back to the counter with Cindy's credit card.

Living It Up- Ann Jennings

When they got back to their room Tori went to show her dad what she had got you're going to be the prettiest one there he said she kissed him then went into the bed room to call Leigh Kay to check on DJ. He's already asleep she told her. I wish I had a brother Leigh Kay said and you have two. Yes and I love them both Tori said even though they can tell when I'm lying or holding a secret but they never tell, my mom can't even tell when I'm lying, mine either Leigh Kay said. Next Tori called Thomas to say goodnight. The next morning the car dealer called Eugene's cell phone and asked him what time he should have the new car delivered and what color ribbon he wanted on it. The graduation was at ten they left the hotel at nine thirty. They couldn't't spot Ronald and didn't see him until they called him to walk across the stage, Dr. Ronald Spellman.

Tori stood and gave a loud cheer for her brother not caring who was looking at her. Ronald look toward her and threw her a kiss. After the ceremony they waited for him in the lobby all the graduates came out a side door and everyone started to applause. Ronald found them and Cindy started to cry. Eugene said let's get out of here. They took Ronald to a very expensive restaurant, a place he had always dreamed of going. The tables were set with glass and Crystal and with more silverware than they knew what to do with.

Living It Up- Ann Jennings

A waiter placed a white starched napkin in their laps and started them off with minestrone soup then after the soup they were served fried cheese sticks next they were served a salad then came the main course. Everyone was served a steak, baked potato and Brussels sprouts cooked with almond slivers. Next came desert something with fire on top but Ronald enjoyed it and to his surprise it wasn't hot next came coffee and then came a glass of wine. Oh my gosh... Ronald said do they offer wheel chair service to the car. Everyone laughed; I can't move Ronald said thank you so much I always pass this place but never thought I would ever get a chance to eat here one day.

You are more than welcome Eugene said you deserve it. The waiter was headed toward their table again with a big white container "Oh no" not again Ronald said, I can't do it. The waiter laughed and placed the container on their table and took the top off, a lot of steam escaped the container then the waiter took tongs and gave them all a steaming hot white cloth to clean their hands. This place is fantastic the service is out of this world and the food is phenomenal Ronald said. The waiter then gave Eugene the bill and Eugene put his credit card into the leather envelop, Ronald was dying to know the cost but was afraid to ask.

Eugene left a generous tip and the waiter walked them to the door and held it open for them. Right in front of the restaurant their car was there for them and the valet was there with the car door open for them to get in. They drove to the airport and turned in the rental car then went to wait for their flight. The only thing Ronald was carrying home with him was a brief case containing his Dr.'s degree his lap top and some more important papers and two bags of dirty clothes.

On the plane ride home Ronald was all talk telling his parents again how much he enjoyed the restaurant and he would love to go back again one day. Did you see how white and starched their jackets were? I have never seen a jacket that white before. When they landed in O'Hair Eugene went to get the Cadillac and told them to wait for the bags and he would be out front with the car. When he got in the car he called Kenny to make sure everything was all set. On the ride home Ronald was all talk telling them about his school, his professors, the food at the school, he couldn't wait to get a home cooked meal not noticing the dark blue car in the drive way with the big yellow bow on top.

Ronald was saying I don't think I would ever be able to afford then he turned his head and spotted the new car in the drive way right in front of them and Kenny was standing beside it smiling. "Oh no" is that mine Ronald said trying to open the door before his dad could come to a complete stop. Are you kidding me he said to his dad, I picked the color Tori said congratulations son Cindy said. Kenny approached his step brother with an extended hand, congratulations brother Kenny said and gave Ronald a hug. Ronald hugged them all and said could he go show it off Kenny tossed him the keys go and have a good time doctor, Eugene said.

Ronald got behind the wheel and Kenny got in on the other side and they drove away. Tori said she was going to Leigh Keys, when she got there DJ was all talk he couldn't stop talking, he told his mom all that him and Auntie Kay did. Mommy I was on the elephant and the giraffe, and the turtle and then I got on the swings not the baby swings the big boy swings then I played in the sand then I got on the slide and the monkey bars Auntie Kay had to hold me up, then "wait" Tori said take a breath. They spent the night and the next morning went to breakfast Tori thanked Leigh Kay and took DJ home.

Tori waited before taking Thomas advice to call and make a doctor's appointment. What are your symptoms the reception asked? Oh just a little dizziness Tori said. Do you think you might be pregnant the receptionist asked? Tori got quiet, ok the doctor can see you at three is that ok? 1:30 would be better Tori said holding hear breath ok I can fit you in at 1:30 she said. Tori let out a breath thanking her so much saying she will be there at 1:30. She was happy that they could see her on her lunch break now no one would know that she was going to the doctor. She called Thomas at school but he didn't answer.

When she looked at the clock on her desk it was only 10:30 he was properly in class. At 1:10 Tori left her office saying she was going to lunch. No one looked up at her so no one noticed how pale she was. Tori's parking spot was close to the door with her name on it. She jumped in her new car Eugene bought her when she started working for him and raced across town and got to the doctor's office at 1:28. The results use to take three days but now they can tell right away. Tori hoped it was the flu but she knew better from past experience. When she walked in Dr. Eto caught his breath, he had forgotten how beautiful she was. So what brings you in today?

Living It Up- Ann Jennings

Tori told him she might be pregnant. When was your last period he asked her? I don't remember she said. Dr. Eto gave Tori a cup and told her to go to the bathroom across the hall and leave a specimen. Write your name on the cup leave it in the little door next to the toilet then have a seat back in the waiting room and he would call her back when he got the results. When Tori went back to the waiting room three ladies were watching a talk show Tori didn't practically like so she picked up a magazine from the table. She thumbed through three magazines without reading one, but smiled when she saw an ad in one for Capable Hands Insurance Company.

Tori had an interminable wait in the Drs. office when she looked up one of the ladies was gone and the nurse was standing at the door calling her name saying Dr. Eto will see you now. The nurse escorted Tori back to the same room she was in earlier. Dr. Eto entered with a single sheet of paper in his hands. Well you were right he said about five weeks. I will start you on prenatal vitamin and you should drink a glass of milk with your meals everyday now cut back on alcohol and no smoking. Start your vitamins today no stress or heavy lifting. Dr. Eto handed Tori her prescription and asked her had she told her parents.

Tori told him she had not but knew she couldn't keep it a secret much longer while giving him a sad look. Well the sooner you tell them the less stress it will be on you and the baby. I'm setting your next appointment for May he said and by then you would have told them because you should be showing by then the second pregnancy is different from the first. Dr. Eto saw Cindy every six months for hormone shots so he knew the next time he saw her she would know of her daughter's condition. Tori rushed back to work without stopping at the pharmacy, if she was a little late going back it would be ok but she didn't want to take advantage of being the boss's daughter.

When she was back in her office she called Thomas again and he answered this time she told him the news. Thomas suggested they tell her parents right away so they decided that evening after dinner was a better time than ever. Tori was glad the rest of her day at the office went slow. She picked DJ up at the day care and he took her mind off the pregnancy by talking a mile a minute, telling her Billy spilled his milk and the teacher gave him a towel and made him wipe it up, but mommy I didn't spill mine DJ said, that's a good boy Tori told him, then he pulled a picture out of his book bag that he had painted and Tori told him it was beautiful.

Thomas showed up after dinner that night while they were still sitting at the table Tori asked him to have desert with them. While Eugene cut into the sweet potato pie Tori told her parents Thomas and she had something to say. Then Thomas pulled a little black box out of his pocket, got on one knee in front of Tori's chair and asked her to marry him in front of her parents. Tori felt her mouth moving but couldn't get the words out right. When? How? What? "Yes Yes" I will she said, Cindy started to cry and Eugene came over to Thomas and shook his hand.

Cindy and Eugene started cleaning up the dinner dishes and left Thomas and Tori alone. This is beautiful Tori told him looking at the ring Thomas put on her finger but you can't afford this. They put me on a payment plain Thomas said smiling. When do we tell them about the "you know" Thomas said looking down at Tori's stomach not now let's let them soak this in first. I already told my mom Thomas said, you did? What did she say? She's the one who took me to the jewelry store to get a ring. Your mom is so sweet I really like her Tori said, she likes you too Thomas said. What do you think Dominique would say Tori asked? He's my friend Thomas said he sees how happy you are with me so I think he'll be happy for us.

What if DJ wants to call you dad? Do you think he would like that too? We'll leave that up to DJ Thomas said. After Thomas left Tori went up to her room to call Leigh Kay. "What?" Are you kidding me he got down on one knee in front of your parents Leigh Kay asked? "Oh" Tori told her you will be having another god-child in eight months. Leigh Kay screamed into the phone are you sure? Did you see a Dr.? Did you tell your mom? Leigh Kay was throwing the questions out so fast Tori couldn't get a chance to answer one. Three months later Tori's mom went way out for the wedding. Dominique was Thomas best man they were still best friends despite the situation.

Dominique had to barrow a suit from Thomas because he didn't own one. Leigh Kay was Tori's maid of honor just like they had planned in fifth grade that they would be each other's maid of honor. The wedding took place on their six acre grounds with all the pretty flowers and tables were set up everywhere they had waiters, chefs and a live band. And a special surprise from Shirley Kenny's ex-girlfriend that knew a friend of Bryan McKnight and asked him if he would sing at the wedding. Tori was a beautiful bride and Thomas was a handsome groom they looked like the perfect couple.

Living It Up- Ann Jennings

The dress Cindy and Leigh Kay picked out for
Tori was perfect for her and Leigh Kay's dress
was a shorter version of Tori's and a lighter
color. The beauty shop had done a good job on
all three girl's hair placing tiny pearls in Tori's
hair to high light her face. They shopped at
four stores before finding the right shoes. The
nail shop polished her nails the same color as
her dress, and arched her eyebrows. Thomas
wore a white tux with an orange shirt the same
color as Tori's dress with white dress shoes.
And Dominique looked very handsome in his
borrowed suit.

Tori and Thomas mom wore large corsages the
color of Tori's dress. All their friends and family
came including employees from Capable
Hands. Thomas old roommates from Florida
came also. Leigh Kay and Cindy helped Tori
into her dress; they had to get a size ten
because her middle wouldn't fit her size eight.
Thomas dressed DJ in his little white tux
Eugene had rented for him. When everyone
was seated the music started to play and Tori
heard Bryan McKnight start to sing her favorite
song. She sat there till her father came for her
and told her it was time.

Living It Up- Ann Jennings

When Tori started to stand she had a pain "Woo" she said holding her stomach. Just take a couple of breaths her dad said I'm sure the baby's probably excited. Tori looked at Eugene, yes we know he said I was just waiting for you to tell me on your own, how long Tori asked? Ever since the proposal your mother took one look at you and she knew. I'm sorry I didn't tell you and mom Tori said. Hey don't you dare cry and mess up that pretty face her father said taking her arm and leading her out while Bryan McKnight sang until Tori and her dad reached the alter.

After a prayer the minister begin, dearly beloved we are gathered here to today to celebrate one of life's greatest moments, to give recognition to the worth and beauty of love, and to add our best wishes to the words which shall unite Thomas and Tori in marriage. Should there be anyone who has cause why this couple should not be united in marriage, they must speak now or forever hold their peace. Who is it that gives this woman to this man? We are Eugene and DJ said in unison just as they had planned it.

Eugene gave Tori's hand to Thomas with a tear in his eye, and then returned to his seat next to Cindy who was already crying. As they faced forward the minister reminded them that life is given to us as individuals, and we must learn to live together. Love is given to us by our family or by our friends. We learn to love by being loved. Learning to love and living together is one of the greatest challenges of life, and is the shared goal of a married life. He then turned to Thomas and asked do you take Tori to be your wife do you promise to love, honor, and cherish and protect her, forsaking all others and holding only until her? I Do Thomas said. Then he turned to Tori, Tori do you take Thomas to be your husband do you promise to love, honor, and cherish and protect him, forsaking all others and holding only until him? I do Tori said in a low voice.

Living It Up- Ann Jennings

As they faced the minister he continued.
Weddings are an outward and visible sign of an
inward spiritual grace and unbroken circle of
love signifying to all the union of this man and
this woman in marriage. The minister asked
Thomas to repeat after him. I Thomas take
Tori to be my wife to have and to hold, in
sickness and health for richer or for poorer,
and I promise my love to you forever. Then he
turned to Tori and had her to repeat the same
words. Then as they faced the minister he
went on to say, Thomas and Tori as the two of
you come into this marriage uniting you as
husband and wife, and as you this day affirm
your faith and love for one another, I would
ask that you always remember to cherish each
other as a special and unique individuals, that
you respect the thoughts, ideas and
suggestions of one another.

He then turned to Tori and said be able to
forgive, and don't hold grudges. Hearing this
everyone knowing Tori laughed. Then he went
on to say live each day that you may share it
together as from this day forward you shall be
each other's home, comfort and refuse, your
marriage strengthened by your love and
respect for one another. After three more
prayers the minister pronounced them
husband and wife. Bryan McKnight started to
sing again. The band started up and the
reception began.

Living It Up- Ann Jennings

Dominique and Tori entered the reception and it was announced, Ladies and gentleman Mr. and Mrs. Middleton will take the first dance. Tori had changed to a shorter orange dress and let her hair down. She dragged her husband onto the dance floor then after the dance they stood there and kissed. Ronald tapped Thomas on the shoulder and asked to dance with his sister; midway through the dance Kenny tapped Ronald on the shoulder and asked to dance with Tori. Everyone started dancing when the band started singing Step by R. Kelly. The next song they sang was a slow song and Shirley brought Bryan McKnight over to dance with Tori.

Tori had a hard time controlling her composure she thought Bryan McKnight was so cute. Leigh Kay was watching her and thought her friend was the prettiest bride she had ever seen. She was glowing and couldn't stop smiling. She had never seen her friend blush until she seen her dance with Bryan McKnight. After her dance he kissed her on the cheek and wished her and Thomas good luck. The band started singing another slow song and Eugene came over and said may I have this dance taking his daughters hand. Are you happy he asked her while they danced; yes daddy I couldn't be happier she told him.

Next they played a game of who knows the bride and groom best, Leigh Kay won for knowing Tori the best even over her own mother and Dominique won for knowing Thomas the best. Trays of champagne and horse d'oeuvres were served by the waiters in all white. The band was taking request and playing everyone's favorite song. The wedding cake had ten layers and around the wedding cake were fifty little personal wedding cakes, a replica of the big one. The ice scripture was breath taking. The dinner was served and everyone took their seats at the beautiful tables that were set up and the waiters started serving the food.

Sheeree told Thomas she had never seen him look so happy. After dinner Tori sat in a chair in the middle of the yard and Thomas removed the orange garter from her thigh and all the guys gathered around and Thomas threw it to them. Then Tori's mom handed her the bouquet and Tori threw it to the group of women. Then the band started up again. By nine that night the reception was still going on but Tori was exhausted. Eugene told her to go and lay down then He told the band to do one more and call it a rap. When Thomas joined Tori in her bed three hours later she turned to her husband and whispered no honey moon tonight.

Living It Up- Ann Jennings

The next day Eugene offered Thomas and Tori the big house and said him and Cindy would move into the guest house. While packing Cindy remembered all the good times they shared in the house with Tori, Ronald and Kenny. Now Thomas and Tori will live there with their growing family only a couple acres away. Life was great after little Eugene was born named after her dad, then only one year later Ronald was born named after her brother. Leigh Kay helped out a lot with the kids, babysitting when Tori and Thomas needed a break.

Dominique's mom even asked Tori to bring DJ over for a visit. Eugene offered Thomas a Vice President position at Capable Hands Insurance after his graduation next year with his degree in business management. Thomas eagerly accepted the offer. Eugene asked Tori would they have more kids? Maybe one more Tori said we would like a daughter.

While having lunch with Leigh Kay one day at a little café down town while Cindy watched the boys, Tori got very sick and Leigh Kay rushed her to the Doctor. The news was just as she expected. On the way home both girls were excited about the pregnancy. Tori told Leigh Kay she wishes she didn't have to go back to school so soon, but she knew how much Leigh Kay wanted to become a surgeon. It won't be long Leigh Kay told her I'll be home before you know it.

After a wonderful lunch the two girls were laughing and singing to the radio and as Leigh Kay drove closer to Tori's house they saw the ambulance and the paramedics bringing a stretcher out. Tori jumped out of the car before Leigh Kay could come to a complete stop and ran into the house to find her mother crying on the couch, when Cindy heard her come in she stretched out her hands to her. Eugene had a heart attack, they tried to save him but they couldn't. The next thing Tori knew they were giving her smelling sauce and she started to cough. Be careful with her she's pregnant Leigh Kay said. For the next two weeks Tori couldn't sleep, couldn't eat couldn't think and couldn't even dress herself.

Living It Up- Ann Jennings

Cindy had to dress her for the funeral and
Thomas had to pick her up and carry her in his
arms into the church. The following month
after the reading of the will Cindy told them
she was moving out of the country that she
couldn't stay in Illinois any more. Eugene had
left all of them comfortable. Tori and Cindy
would receive a generous amount each month
from the company which was left to Thomas.
Ronald and Kenny was left a generous lump
sum, the property was left to Cindy who in turn
signed it over to Tori and Thomas.

After seven months Tori gave birth to triplets,
the first two boys were normal but the third
boy was oxygen deficient and had brain
damage and was told that he would be special.
Lawrence was the first triplet to be born
weighing five pounds, then two minutes later
Richard was born weighing five pounds; Mickey
was born seven minutes later weighing only
two pounds. As infant's Lawrence was always
the strongest of the three. He was the first to
sit up by himself, the first to crawl, the first to
get a tooth and the first to say daddy.

Living It Up- Ann Jennings

It was like he was telling his brothers "don't do anything unless I do it first." Richard would always do what his older brother did three weeks later. And Mickey never caught up. Lawrence told Richard that he would never be better than him. Tori would dress all three boys' alike but different colors. Lawrence would spill milk or syrup on his clothes so his mother would have to change his clothes. Eugene and Ronald knew what he was doing but never told their mother. I don't like dressing like them Lawrence told his two older brothers. Tori would always bath all three boys together and they would put all their little toys into the tub with them.

Then when they turned three Lawrence told her he didn't want to take a bath with his brother's anymore. He wanted to take a bath by himself like DJ, Ronald and Eugene. Then at four he told her he wanted his own room. Eugene was one year older than Ronald and three years older than the triplets. Four months later Cindy moved to sunny Bahamas, Thomas was working twelve hours a day, and Leigh Kay was away at school and Tori felt that her world had come to an end.

Living It Up- Ann Jennings

Eight months later after trying to be the good wife to Thomas at night, listening to the boy's fighting all day, house work, washing two loads of laundry a day, Tori came to the conclusion she couldn't do it anymore. When Thomas came home late again that night from work Tori had her bags packed at the front door and told Thomas she was leaving, Thomas stood there stunned. Tori continued please don't try to stop me, things are moving too fast for me, I have never had a life of my own, I had DJ in high school, then I married you and had five more kids, I need time for me. He asked if she had called her mother, at the same time they heard the cab blowing the horn outside.

Living It Up- Ann Jennings

No I have not called her but I'm sure you will. After the cab pulled off he did just that. Cindy was living it up in the Bahamas; Thomas woke her and thought he heard a male's voice in the background. She promised him she would talk to her and to give her a few days. But how am I going to work and take care of six kids Thomas shot back. Cindy said she would hire him a sitter from her end. The next day when DJ came home from school Thomas told him his mom had left them, why DJ asked? I don't know Thomas told him she just said she had enough. DJ didn't take the news to well; he announced he was going to live with his dad. Thomas told him his dad still lived with his mom in a two bedroom apartment and managed a gas station.

Well I'm going DJ screamed running up to pack his clothes. Tom called Dominique and told him his son's plans. I cant take care of no kid Dominique said, I'm never home and mom drinks too much. Well I have five here to take care of and I can't stop him Thomas said. That evening DJ left and took all his clothes. Eugene wanted to go with his brother but Thomas had to explain to him that he had to stay with him. The next day a house keeper showed up from Nanny Services saying Cindy Spellman had hired her.

Thomas introduced her to the kids and they loved her except for Eugene. Cindy came the next month to visit her grandson's and to check on the house keeper she was paying every month. She only stayed for four day's saying she had appointments and had to get back. Eugene begged her to take him back with her, she explained to him she only had one bed room and in a no kids community. Tori called once a month and every time she did Thomas begged her to come back and he always got the same answer. I'm sorry but I can't come back to that life any more.

Living It Up- Ann Jennings

She lived in California, had a mansion bought by her married lover and he found out from Leigh Kay she was having the time of her life. He didn't tell her that the kid's grades were falling since she left them. According to Leigh Kay, Tori was giving parties every weekend, shopping on an unlimited charge card every week end, massages three times a week, hair and nails done every four days, and Leigh Kay even told Tom she got her shape back and looked like a million bucks, a little too much makeup but she looked good. Leigh Kay told Thomas each time she would go to California to visit her she would take her on shopping sprees buying her the most expensive clothes and jewelry. And the parties she threw in her home were incredible with all the rappers, R&B singers, movie stars and top officials and she even got to hang out with Bryan McKnight again, she hadn't seen him since her wedding.

Living It Up- Ann Jennings

Tori always took Leigh Kay to the most exclusive restaurants in California for lunch, and it was always then that Leigh Kay asked her if she was ready to come home. Tori's answer was always the same. Then one time she asked Leigh Kay if she would move to California to be with her. Thomas asked Leigh Kay please don't move to California, my kids are crazy about you and I was hoping you would stay here and marry me. Leigh Kay stared at Thomas as if he was transparent. Thomas repeated what he said; will you marry me Leigh Kay? Eight years ago this would have been a dream come true, but now I'm afraid it's too late.

 Leigh Kay stayed and helped Thomas bathe the boys and read them a story. When she got home her mother noticed the worried look on her daughters face and asked her if she wanted to talk. She told her parents what Thomas had asked her. Leigh Kay's mom was furious, she got up and stormed across the room saying "Definitely Not" you will not marry him and raise six kids that's not yours and you tell him I said you will be going back to school to become a surgeon, either you tell him or I will.

Living It Up- Ann Jennings

Her classes started back in three days; she would spend two days in Hollywood California with Tori and attend the Academy Awards, which she had never dreamed she would ever go to such an event. Tori bought her a gown costing over five thousand dollars. Where am I going to wear this again Leigh Kay asked her. Leigh Kay was having the time of her life shaking hands with some of her famous singer's and movie stars. The next night Tori drove her friend to Los Angeles International Air Port. Leigh Kay didn't like the fast life Tori was living but she was her best friend and always would be.

The sitter Cindy hired for Thomas and the boys didn't work out. She had no patience for Mickey so Sheeree Tom's mom came to live with them. Thomas cut his hours down to eight hours a day to spend more time with his mom and the boy and to help out with Mickey who was five but still had the mental capacity of a six month old. DJ continued to live with his father and grandmother spending most days alone with no food. Eugene, Ronald and the triplets loved grandma living there with them; Eugene has never asked to go live with his brother again. Cindy called and said she was getting married again. Tori was still living the fast life in Hollywood California and loving it, the kids don't ask about her as much anymore.

Living It Up- Ann Jennings

Tori's brother Dr. Ronald Spellman left the hospital he was working at and opened his own practice. Kenny's Style and Cut, was the hottest barber shop in town, he and his girlfriend Shirley also became a record producer. When the triplets started school their brother Eugene was in the fourth grade and Ronald was in the third grade. Lawrence told his dad he would not go to the same school as Mickey. Since the triplets were born Lawrence wanted no part of his brother Mickey, he would not look at him or talk to him, and when Mickey cried Lawrence would cover his ears.

Once when Sheeree had water boiling on the stove Mickey was reaching up trying to touch it when his brother Richard walked into the kitchen and ran to stop him while Lawrence sat at the table watching him not saying a word. "Didn't you see him" his brother Richard scolds his older brother? Yes I saw him was all Lawrence said and got up and walked out of the kitchen.

Living It Up- Ann Jennings

Dominique never wanted to go back to live with Thomas and his brothers, the house reminded him too much of his mom. In ninth grade he was raising himself, coming and going when he wanted, drinking and doing drugs with friends until he met Jan during that summer after he finished ninth grade. He had already made up his mind that he was not going back to school, no matter how much Jan begged, his answer was still no. After two years, in Jan's second year of high school she was still trying to get Dominique to come back to school. It's too late for me now he would tell her; you just get your diploma, go to college and make me proud.

Jan decided not to ride the bus home and walk the eight block's home from school not noticing the two degree temperature. Her mind was on Dominique and the conversation they had last night. During school she didn't hear a word her teachers said, she just couldn't believe Dominique would hurt her like that. She couldn't wait to get home to call her best friend Marvaleen, who went to a different school from her and two years older. Marvaleen was the only one she could talk to right now and the only one that could calm her down. When Jan entered her house her mom asked where's your gloves? Jan replied in my pocket not looking at her mom while racing up to her room.

Living It Up- Ann Jennings

Isn't your hands cold her mom called up the
stairs. Jan entered her room and closed the
door. After two years she never thought her
and Dominique would break up. Jan thought
her and Dominique would get married one day
but now he told her he wanted to explore,
whatever that means. Jan was his first
girlfriend and he was her first boyfriend for two
years they were happy and Jan thought things
were going great. Jan picked up the phone and
called Marvaleen to get some comfort. When
Marvaleen answered she could hear the hurt in
her friends voice, I'll be right over Marvaleen
told her. When she arrived at Jan's she was
not prepared to see her friend so pale, they
talked quietly for hours in Jan's room.

Living It Up- Ann Jennings

After Marvaleen calmed Jan down some she
told her it will get better, that she and
Dominique have had disagreements before and
gotten through it. This is just another one of
those hurdles that you will go though. That's
what I love about you two you always settle
your arguments and go right back to being
lovie dovie. Not this time Jan said starting to
cry again. You say the same thing every time
Marvaleen said, but in the end you two always
work it out. Jan's mom brought up snacks but
Jan couldn't eat anything. Do you mind
Marvaleen asked Jan picking up a sandwich
from the plate and stuffing it in her mouth,
then picking up one of the two bottles of coke
taking a big gulp, you should eat something
she told Tori picking up another sandwich.

Living It Up- Ann Jennings

The next morning Jan decided to walk to school again not feeling the cold; she had decided to let Dominique go, this would be the hardest thing she ever had to do. This was something she had to do in order to move on with her life because she couldn't live like this. She didn't want to give up without a fight but Dominique seemed to be so sure of himself when they talked. Going to parties, skating and the movies won't be the same without Dominique Jan thought. The way they skate together was magical. Everyone would watch them skate around the floor doing their dance, and Dominique would throw in a flip, everyone would clap and say "do it again."

Jan was day dreaming the next day during algebra class glazing out the window at the bare trees, the day seemed gloomy as she remembered the last time her and Dominique went to the movies and the way they laughed and ate popcorn out of one bucket and shared a coke. At that moment Mrs. Smith was at Jan's desk asking her did she know the answer to the question jolting Jan from her daydream "Oh, I, UM" no mam. Did you do your homework Ms. Peters?

"No, she was dreaming about her boyfriend Dominique", someone called out from the back of the room. Then someone stated making kissing noises and all the boys started laughing. After algebra class Jan decided to skip the rest of her classes for the day and go to the park to weigh her options. Suicide was one of her options then quickly dismissed because her mom would never be the same and would never forgive her. She was always told suicide was the biggest sin of all and God would never forgive her for taking her own life also she would not be welcome into Heaven.

Then she thought about running away. But her mom would have the Chicago Police to find her and bring her back. She thought about her dad, he would take her but he live so far away, and she would miss her mom. Even though her dad has only lived in Canada for one year she was sure he had found someone else, then it came to her. When Jan got home the next day she called Marvaleen to tell her that she was tired of fighting and had made her final decision. Marvaleen told her to wait before she make that final decision, let Jesus and I talk to Dominique first she said. Jesus was Marvaleen's boyfriend and in his first year at the University of Illinois.

Living It Up- Ann Jennings

The senior picnic is coming up in three weeks and I will ask one of the other seniors to invite Dominique. Even though Dominique was fifteen Jan knew he would be thrilled to be asked to the senior picnic by a seventeen year old. When Lynn a class mate of Marvaleen's asked Dominique to the picnic he was thrilled and accepted. Dominique knew Lynn and her twin sister Linda and had always admired them. Dominique bragged to his friends about going to the picnic with the twins sticking his chest out. He did odd jobs to buy him a nice outfit for the picnic. He was surprised when Lynn asked him, not knowing that Marvaleen had asked her to ask him so she could talk to him alone.

Three weeks later at the senior picnic Dominique felt like a big shot having no idea that Marvaleen and Jesus was going to ambush him. When they finally got a chance to talk to him he was having so much fun with all the senior girl's telling them he had a girlfriend but he felt smothered and just wanted to explore a little. Jesus understood but this made Marvaleen mad even though she thought Dominique looked happier than she had ever seen him.

Living It Up- Ann Jennings

He was only fifteen years old like Jan and only two years younger than her and he had been through so much. The next day Marvaleen had to tell Jan the news that she did not want to hear. Early Sunday morning Jan called Marvaleen before she even got up. Marvaleen told her she was going to come over as soon as she got up, what time is it anyway Marvaleen asked? Six thirty Jan said. So did you and Jesus get to talk to Dominique? I'm sorry, Jan Jesus and I tried. Its ok Jan said, thanks for trying and thank Jesus for me too she was tired of fighting.

Jan lay in her bed quietly until she heard her mom get up she went into her mom's room and told her she wanted to accept the invitation to the Jones Commercial All girl Business Academy for the gifted. She was accepted there when school started but turned it down to stay close to home and Dominique. At that time she couldn't see herself going down town to school and not having Dominique waiting outside the school when she got out walking her home and sometimes stopping at the park on the way home or to get an ice cream cone.

Living It Up- Ann Jennings

The next morning Mrs. Peters started the paper work for her daughter. Now instead of taking the school bus Jan had to take public transportation down town to school giving up her fashion jeans and designer boots for skirts and hills. At Jones Commercial business Academy suits was the attire every day. In May of that year Jan attended Marvaleen's graduation, she decided not to go to dinner with them afterwards to give them time alone. That summer when school let out Jan kelp herself busy by helping her mom around the house doing laundry and running errands.

On the hot summer nights her and her mom would sit on the porch talking and counting the stars, a game they played often. Her and her mom became best friends, she wish she would have meet Dominique's mom but he never talked about her. Jan and her mom would laugh about the things she did when she was a little girl. Remember when you told me you were going to marry Mr. Washawsky her mom said? Oh yes I was only in third grade Jan said, I wish I would have wrote all that down her mom said. At the end of summer Mrs. Peters took Jan shopping for new clothes for her new school.

Living It Up- Ann Jennings

At the mall Jan picked out two plaid skirts she really liked, with a big buckle on the side and pleats. The next weekend they went to the out-let mall and Jan found two cute blouses to match her skirts. On the way home they stopped at a little café for lunch. They both ordered salad with baby shrimps and lemon aid; after they finished their salad they shared a slice of cake. On the ride home Jan asked her mom "what if I don't meet any friends?" Oh honey I'm sure you'll meet plenty of new friends at your new school. You just have that killer face; they both busted out laughing when Mrs. Peters made a funny face.

That night Jan talked to Marvaleen and told her the same thing she told her mom. Well I guess I'll just have to be your best and only friend for the rest of your life Marvaleen said. No I'm serious Jan said, what if the girls don't like me? I'm sure they'll love you Marvaleen said you'll see. Hey Jan said, want to go shopping with me and my mom next weekend we only have one more weekend for shopping before school starts, and I still have a ton of things to get. Ok that sounds fun Marvaleen said just let me know what time Saturday and you know I like to sleep late, yes I know Jan said with sarcasm. You're going to sleep your life away, sounds good to me Marv said in fact I think I'll start now "good night."

Living It Up- Ann Jennings

Mrs. Peters drove Jan everyday her first week at Jones Commercial Academy. Then Jan started to meet new friends and started catching the city bus with them. Jan exchanged phone numbers with three girls at school so if it was something she didn't understand she could call them. All the girls there got along well together. The school was run like a business instead of a school; you would clock in ever day then clock out for lunch if you leave the campus. The food in the cafeteria was very good; usually everyone would stay at school and eat.

At Jones Commercial everyone had to be greeted by Mr. or Miss. And their last name Jan couldn't see her friend Jasmine Shakir in the halls and say "hey Jas" she had to say hello Miss. Shakir and Jasmine had to say hello Miss. Peters. On those bitter cold mornings in November Mrs. Peters would drive Jan to school and was there to pick her up at two. Some days when Jan would walk out the school she missed seeing Dominique standing there waiting for her with a big smile on his face, he would take her book bag which now everyone at Jones Commercial had to carry black brief cases and he would walk her home. Jan would miss out on the proms because at Jones Commercial there was no prom, everything was all about business.

Living It Up- Ann Jennings

Jan's junior year went better than she had predicted it, she met lots of friends and all her teachers liked her. She thought it would be hard going to a school with all girls but it went well. That summer she and Marvaleen hung out a lot and when she wasn't with Marvaleen she was at home with her mom. When classes started back in September she was happy to be in her last year. One day in one of Jan's classes her teacher told them owners of companies will be coming to their school to show the students how to conduct their selves at an interview. The companies will come in and interview the student's and that they would need to write a résumé and cover letter to present to the interviewer.

That evening Jan told her mom she was nerves, she had never been on an interview before. I'm sure you'll do great Mrs. Peters said just dress nice and don't chew gum, that's not a problem Jan said we can't chew gum at school anyway. Jan went up to her room to call Marvaleen and tell her about the interview at school the next day Marvaleen's reassured her telling her the same thing her mom had said. Oh and one more thing Marvaleen told her try not to sweat. That night Jan and her mom was on the computer eating a pizza her mom had delivered until after eleven writing a resume and cover letter.

Living It Up- Ann Jennings

The next morning Jan dressed in a black business suit, white blouse and black pumps with coffee stockings and a business hat and when she grabbed her briefcase her mom told her she looked like she was off to work. Mrs. Peters drove Jan to school that morning. First and second period went great for Jan but when then it was time for third period class her and all her friends were nervous about the interviews. When they walked into the class room the teacher was not sitting behind her desk instead she was sitting in the back of the room and there was a man sitting there in a three piece suit and a big lather chair sitting in front of the desk and a sign on the desk saying Chicago Tribune human resource.

After everyone was seated the teacher asked who wanted to go first. No one raised their hand so the teacher picked who she wanted to go first Jan was hoping she didn't pick her. At the end of the interviews it was time for the girls to go to fourth period class. The teacher was talking to the man from the Chicago Tribune when they left the room and Jan wondered what they were talking about. Jan couldn't wait until the next day to see how she did. When she got home she called Marvaleen and told her about the interview, I was so nervous she told her and my knees were shaking, but I didn't sweat.

I'll know my grade tomorrow she told her. Jan didn't sleep good that night this interview would be part of her finial grade and at Jones Commercial and only "A" grades were accepted at Jones Commercial she had heard of a couple of girls who's grades fell below an "A" and had to be sent back to their regular high school. The next morning Jan took the bus down town to school she had to take off her boots and put her hills on and take off the pants which she wore under her skirt to keep her legs worm before she could enter the school and put them in a bag which all the girls did that rode the bus on cold mornings.

Living It Up- Ann Jennings

During first and second period class she kept looking at her watch. After second period she walked slowly to her third period class. There was a crowed of girls looking at the board outside the class room. All the girls names were on the board with a grade in all categories, Jan didn't know they were testing them on everything. Beside the board was a list if you wanted to retake the interview you had to sign your name on the list. They graded you on first how you approached the desk, then if you greeted the interviewer and shook his hand, your posture as you sat in the chair, they were taught to sit at the front of the chair with their back's and one foot in front of the other, your dress and appearance, your speech, they wanted to see if you were chewing gum, your concentration, your answers to questions and how you would be a big asset to the company if hired and how you got up to leave, and if you thanked the interviewer and shook hand.

Living It Up- Ann Jennings

Each interview lasted ten minutes; Jan finally got to the front of the crowd and found her name. Her scores were 90, 90, 90, 70, 100, 100, 70, 90, 100, 90, 90, and 90. Jan saw all the mistake's she had made and signed her name on the list next to the board to take the interview over again. Jan saw Jasmine in the crowd of girls signing up to redo the interview and said hello Miss. Shakir are you signing up again? Yes jasmine said me too Jan said now that I know what all they look for, I didn't think I did that bad until I looked at my scores Jan said, me too Jasmine said.

Jasmine said you know next week we will be going to visit colleges, no I didn't know Jan said I haven't checked my box lately. Two weeks later Jan and her mom wrote up a better résumé and cover letter printing it out on silk printing paper and putting it in a see through folder. The next day after second period Jan rushed to her third period class and was the one who raised her hand when her third period teacher asked who wanted to go first.

The next day all the girl's passed with 100%. The two years at Jones Commercial went by quickly Jan meet lots of friends and graduated at the top of her class. By the time Jan graduated Marvaleen was pregnant and planning her wedding to Jesus. Jan thought of Dominique every once in a while and heard he had started drinking again. Dominique would often see his brother Lawrence always with a different girl and would run away before Lawrence noticed him; he did not want his brother to see him in that condition.

Jan wanted to take a year off before starting college but her mom advised her not to. So she gave into her mother's wishes and got a full scholar ship for the first four years to become a Veterinarian; which would take at least five or six years to complete. She had to know every bone, every muscle, every vain, every nerve from front to back on every animal and how every organ worked. That's why she wanted to take a year off to rest her brains because she knew once she started she couldn't take a break.

Living It Up- Ann Jennings

She would spend the first four years at Georgia State University to start her studies. Her mom gave her a big party before she had to leave for Georgia. All her friends from her old high school and Jones Commercial came and lot of her teachers came also. The next day after the party the grant papers came via first class mail, alone with channel 2, 5, and 7 news trucks. As she sat at her kitchen table signing paper's the news announcer was saying to the camera, Congratulations go out to Ms. Jan Peters for accepting a four year scholar ship to Georgia State University to start her journey to become the first African American to receive a scholar ship to become a Veterinarian.

After signing the paper's they turned to Jan and asked her if she would like to say a word or two. Knowing this was all her mom's doing she started out by thanking her mom then thanked Georgia State for believing in her and giving her the scholar ship, and then Jones Commercial for preparing her. Jan had to leave in two weeks. Not knowing what classes to take first Jan was worried until a package came in the mail with her full agenda for the first semester listing all her classes, teachers, room numbers, the dates for the finials and a generous check for books and clothing allowance.

Living It Up- Ann Jennings

Jan's life was going so fast at this point she didn't have time to even take a deep breath. But one thing she did know, she wasn't going anywhere until after the wedding. Two weeks later Mrs. Peters and Jan went to Georgia State to take a tour of the College. The campus was nothing like Jan had imagined. It was like a city in its self. After the tour they went to find Jan's dorm. The room was small, two small beds, two small windows, two small desks, and two small closets with a key sticking out of one.

Jan's mother pulled out her tape measure and started measuring the window for curtains. She could already see that the bed was bunk size. As they started to leave a very tall distinguish looking girl rushed in almost knocking them down. Jan's mom was the first to speak. The girl introduced herself as Sophy Daniels from Indianapolis Indiana and a junior. Well maybe you girls can come home together Indiana is only two hours from us. I don't go home Sophy said I don't have a car and my parents don't own one.

Jan's mom wasn't ready for Jan to have a car yet because she liked driving her around. So when was the last time you saw your parents Jan's mom asked Sophy. It was at the awards ceremony they gave for the freshmen's when we went from freshman to sophomore. After throwing her bag on her bed Sophy told them she had to run. She told them she worked in the library every day after class until nine when the library closed. On her way out the door she told Jan "Oh the bath room is right down the hall on the right." Jan told her she wasn't staying but she would be back to start classes next week.

Sophy closed the door behind her running down the hall. Jan and her mom looked at each other at the same time the door close and said in unison "that was weird. "On the way home they stopped to buy a bed in a bag for Jan's bed and window, and a small rug to go in front of her bed. Jan picked up a gift for Marvaleen and Jesus. Their wedding was next Saturday and Jan would leave the following day to start classes on Monday. The following day after they got back from Georgia Marvaleen called in a panic telling Jan she had to go with her to buy another dress for the wedding, the one she was going to wear she bought it too soon and now it's too tight.

They spent the entire day out going to three different malls until they found what they wanted. Marvaleen had to get a size 18 to fit her and the baby. They went to McDonalds in the mall and ate chicken nuggets before going home. The next Saturday Jan walked into the small church and was surprised at how beautiful it was. Marvaleen had done a great job on the decorations. She and Jesus paid for everything themselves except for the large pot of flowers that Jan bought for them and Marvaleen's bouquet Jan's mom made for them.

Marvaleen and Jesus were both loners. They never asked anyone for anything, whatever they needed or wanted they got it on their own, or went without. They both came from very poor families. Marvaleen's family sometimes ate rice for months but was grateful because at least it was hot and they could always eat as much as she wanted. All the toy's she got was always from the second hand store or found by her father in an alley after someone's child had gotten tired of playing with it and threw it out.

Living It Up- Ann Jennings

Marvaleen's first bike came from the goodwill
and after her dad fixed the front wheel and
chain it was like new and he was only out of a
dollar for it. Marvaleen's mother would always
tell her things will get better one day, but that
day never came. She still had to struggle for
what she needed. Marvaleen was embarrassed
to invite people over to their apartment
because of the holes in the wall's and the
pealing ceiling. When Jan came over to visit
they would sit on the porch or in Marvaleen's
room, which she tried to fix up despite the
damage to the wall's which she covered with
posters. But she did have good music; her dad
had found a perfectly good entertainment
center and an old stereo in the trash and
brought it home to Marvaleen.

Sometimes Jan and Marvaleen would sit in her
room for hour's listening to their favorite
music. Jan would always bring snacks when
she came over. Marvaleen was always
comfortable around Jan from the first time
they meet when Marvaleen was a freshman in
high school and Jan was in seventh grade. She
would always call her, her little sister.
Marvaleen meet Jesus in high school, their
lockers were next to each other, she would
sometimes leaving little note's on his locker
saying have a good day, or do you want to sit
at my table and eat lunch together.

Living It Up- Ann Jennings

Jesus didn't have many friends either because he didn't wear the latest fashions, but Marvaleen thought he was the cutest Mexican she had ever seen. Jesus family was on welfare all his life. He remember going to the grocery store with his mom and her paying with food stamps. They always had food in the house but never enough money. The building they lived in was run down on the outside but decent on the inside.

Their lights were cut off a lot and they had no hot water. When his parent's couldn't pay the light bill Jesus stayed out late at a friends until it was time for bed then went home to a dark house and got under the cover's to keep warm. And in the morning he would get food stamps from his mother and run to the gas station down the street to buy hot chocolate before going to school. He would be warm all day at school, but when school was over he would dread going home to the cold house.

His grades were too good for him to have to stay after for help that's how he got the job at the Boys and Girls club tutoring the kid's that was having trouble keeping up in school, that's where he met Dominique and introduced him to Jan. Jesus family didn't have a phone at home they would use the one at the gas station down the street. For Jesus birthday his mom would fix all his favorite foods for him and the same for Christmas. Jesus always said to himself "One day I'm going to be someone special." Jan took her place up front next to Jesus and the minister then Marvaleen's dad walked her down the aisle.

After the wedding was a reception down stairs in the room they use for Sunday school. It was decorated with pink and black balloons, a small table was set up with a small wedding cake and finger sandwiches'. Marvaleen cut the first piece of cake and fed it to her husband. Then they went to the dance floor while Jan took over cutting the cake for the guest. Every time she would cut a piece of cake and put it on the small plate someone would take it. Then a voice behind her said make mines a double.

Jan turned around and looked into the most loving eyes. All she could say was Dominique, what are you doing here? I mean when did you? Dominique stopped her by taking both her hands and squeezing them. If I make you uncomfortable I can leave Dominique said Jan went back to fumbling her words. No please, I mean don't, um... stay, Um... Jesus and Marv just got married. I know Dominique said laughing still holding her hands. "Wow" you look great Jan he said, it's been a long time since I've seen you.

Jan finally found her voice and said, "I leave for college tomorrow" and before she could get all the words out Dominique said I'll wait for you, no matter how long it takes. Jan got someone else to serve the cake. Marvaleen and Jesus were still on the dance floor. She and Dominique found a table in the corner of the room. So you're finally going to become a Vet Dominique said, it's been your dream since grade school. Remember the injured squeal we found in your back yard? Yes Jan said I finally gave up trying to save it and asked my mom to rush me to the Vet with it. I'm glad they were able to save it Dominique said, yes me too Jan said. They both looked away at Marvaleen and Jesus on the dance floor.

Marvaleen was the prettiest bride Jan had ever seen. She was smiling and seemed so happy, Jan wish she would be as happy as her on her wedding day. Jan's beautician had done a nice job on Marvaleen's hair and makeup, another one of Jan's wedding gifts to her. Dominique, Jan said, the last time we argued, I'm still not ready. I had a long talk with Jesus and I understand now Dominique said, you're not like those other girls, and I'm sorry I pressured you, and I appreciate you more now for turning me down all those years. I'm so sorry baby would you forgive me Dominique said.

Yes I think I can manage that Jan said. You can follow your dream too Dominique Jan said. Dominique thought this would be a good time to tell Jan his secrete. Not only did he not go back to school but he started hanging out with the wrong crowed and started doing bad thing's. Dominique told her the whole story, even about his encounter with the twin's. When the music stopped Marvaleen and Jesus saw the two of them talking and decided to leave them alone.

After an hour of talking to Jan and telling her all the bad thing's he's been doing he was crying. Its ok Jan said, while I'm away at school you can get your GED and take some college course's. Marvaleen came to the table and took both their hands; ok, you guys are too serious over here, this is a party not a funeral, "let's dance" Marvaleen said dragging them to the dance floor. After the reception Jan sent Marvaleen and Jesus home saying her and Dominique would clean up. Jan's mom said she would come back in an hour to take her and Dominique home.

 After Dominique helped Jesus take all their wedding gifts to the car he and Jan talked quietly while cleaning. Jan's mom returned in an hour and dropped Dominique off at home on their way home. The following day was hard for Jan, she ask her mom if Dominique could ride with them to Georgia, which she agreed. During the long ride Jan and Dominique sat in the back seat and played games. When they reached the college Dominique helped Jan and her mom take all Jan's things up to her dorm room. They stayed as long as they could, Jan's mom was exhausted. She would get a good night's sleep before heading back.

Living It Up- Ann Jennings

Mrs. Peters gave her daughter a long hug and told Dominique she would wait for him in the car. It was hard for Dominique to let go but he knew he had to go. He still remembered when he came home from school and Thomas told him that his mom had left them. He loved his mom so much and she left him, now it's happening all over again with Jan.

The next morning on the long ride home Mrs. Peters and Dominique did not talk much. When Mrs. Peters got to Dominique's apartment she turned to him and said "She's living her dream you know, Please don't bring her down" she's wanted this all her life, I know said Dominique I promise I won't do anything to get in her way. She really loves you, you know? And I love her too Dominique said. And you have my word I will encourage her every chance I get, thank you so much Mrs. Peters said she needs it.

While Jan was away at college Mrs. Peters had too much time on her hands, than she knew what to do with it. As far back as she can remember she had always wanted to foster kids, not just any kid's but older ones left in foster care only to be put out at age twenty one. These are the ones she felt sorry for. She had always wanted to adopt twins, or a sister and brother or two brothers or two sisters.

Living It Up- Ann Jennings

She wanted to be the one that say's don't separate the children I'll take them all. It break's her heart to see brother's and sister's being separated. She wanted more laughter in the house, she wanted to cook for more than one, she wanted to go to the grocery store and fill a grocery cart up with food instead of using a basket, she wanted to talk to someone across the table and say how was your day, she wanted to put candle's on a birthday cake and say make a wish and blow out the candles.

 All these things she misses doing. She looked the number up for foster care and dialed the number, Mrs. Pitts told her she would have to come in a fill out a twenty five page application, and read off a long list of paper's Mrs. Peters needed to bring with her, from the list she read off Mrs. Peters said I may as well bring my whole file cabinet, just about Mrs. Pitts laughed, then there will be three home visits and one surprise visit and all this will take about a year to complete a whole year Mrs. Peters said? Yes Mrs. Pitts said you will have six months of classes.

Living It Up- Ann Jennings

What are the classes for Mrs. Peters asked I already know how to raise kids, yea I understand but it's procedure's Mrs. Pitts said. Everyone says that but these kids are different they're angry that they can't live with their real parent's for whatever reason and they're withdrawn and act up a lot. Mrs. Peters made an appointment to fill out the application the next day. Filling out the application took most of the day and the following day the agency showed up for a home visit she was nerves when they came into her house but after the ladies were seated on her sofa they were so nice her nervousness went away fast.

They were laughing and drinking coffee like old friend's they told her most people only want babies' and no one want's the older kid's, but Mrs. Peters assured them that she did not want a baby. At Mrs. Peters first class they showed films of African American children in foster homes that needed a home. Innocent kid's with no hope's and dream's, they only wanted someone to love and someone to love them, Mrs. Peters didn't know she was crying until a tear fell down and hit her arm.

Living It Up- Ann Jennings

Two months later they showed up again without calling. After they left this time Mrs. Peters had not heard from the agency for six and a half months. Then Mrs. Peters phone rang at three in the morning thinking it was Jan she rushed to pick it up. The adoption agency was calling to see if she would take in three brothers' whose parents were just killed in a plane crash. Mrs. Peters told them to bring the boy's over, she got up and put the coffee pot on then turned on the TV in the kitchen. Perry, Percy and Parnell Gibbs didn't know why they were being taken away from their aging grandparent's.

The police was talking quietly with their grandparent's and Perry saw his grandmother crying. A kind lady asked them to gather some of their clothes and their favorite toy that she was taking them with her. But what about Grandma Perry said, why is grandma crying Parnell said, where are we going Percy said? To a place where you'll meet lots of friend's the lady said, I like my old friends Parnell said. Our parents are coming back today and we will be going home Perry said. The policeman that was talking to his grandmother in the living room walked into the room and said "hi boy's" Perry read the name on his badge which said McCoy. What's your name the officer asked I'm Perry these are my brother's Percy and Parnell.

Living It Up- Ann Jennings

My name is Lionel the officer said. Why is our grandma crying Percy said? She would like to talk to you three in the other room Lionel said. The three boys' ran to their grandparent's and now their grandfather was crying also holding their grandmother. What's wrong Perry said why these people here are in the middle of the night. You know your parent's were coming back today their grandfather started off saying well their plane went down then his grandfather was crying so hard he couldn't finish so Lionel McCoy had to give the boy's the bad news a job he never got used to doing.

Now I need for you to go with the nice lady, I'll stay here with your grandparent's and I won't leave them until I think they're ok. All three boys were crying and holding on to each other. The caseworker had packed their things and was waiting for them at the front door. Did you pack my blanket Parnell said, he never goes anywhere without his blanket Perry said. It's the tricolor one Perry said; Perry went back into the room to retrieve the blanket. Are we coming back Parnell asked, mom won't know where we are, she's not coming back Perry said.

"Yes she is" Percy said you don't know what you're talking about. The three boy's stated hitting each other until Lionel had to break them up. One hour later they were pulling up to Mrs. Peters home, when she saw them pull up she ran to open the door. Perry and Percy were walking next to the case worker who was carrying Parnell who had fallen asleep. The caseworker helped Mrs. Peters put the boys to bed then went into the kitchen to talk. The caseworker told her all the information she needed to know for now, and one more thing she said on her way out it would be all over the news tomorrow so you might not want to let the boys watch TV or listen to the radio when they wake.

She called Jan and told her that she was fostering three brothers ages 7, 8 and 10. That's nice Jan said I didn't know you had took foster classes. "Oh Jan you would love them" her mom sang into the phone. What's their name Jan asked? Perry, Percy and Parnell Gibbs her mom said. It had been a long time since Jan heard her mom sound so happy. The boy's had brought so much joy to her life although they argued a lot among themselves she still enjoyed the company she also enjoyed cooking for them and reading to them at night she enjoyed having someone to watch a good movie with her on TV and they were very helpful around the house even though she never asked them to lift the finger.

Living It Up- Ann Jennings

Jan came home for the Labor Day weekend by Gray Hound; she didn't want her mom on the road during the holiday. The three day's at home went well; she spent her days with her mom and her night's talking quietly to Dominique on her mom's couch. She told him about her classes, and her professors. It's like high school but only the professor's don't look over your shoulder all the time like in high school. And you could just get up and walk out in the middle of class without asking. And the most important is you can eat and drink and chew gum right there at your desk while the professor is teaching they don't care as long as you don't disrespect your class mate's it's totally independent. The next time she came home for Thanks Giving Jan got to meet the foster kid's that her mom had told her about. Mrs. Peters invited Marvaleen, Jesus and Dominique to have dinner with them.

Marvaleen told Jan the next time you come home you will get to meet your god child, our god child Dominique said I want to be part of the child's life too. We will take him to the park and put him in gymnastics Dominique said and teach him to follow his dream Jan said. Wait a minute Marvaleen said how do you know it's going to be a boy? It'll be a boy Jesus said; I know little JJ will be a worrier. After dinner Jan and Marvaleen helped Mrs. Peters put things away. After everything was done Jan and Dominique went back to Marvaleen and Jesus apartment to hang out while listening to music and snacking on some of the left over's Mrs. Peters sent home with them.

They did this every day that week, they spent the day's with Mrs. Peters and the boy's, taking the boys to movies to the park and out for ice cream and the night's with Marvaleen and Jesus. On the last night the four of them stayed up all night talking. Jesus drove Jan to the Gray Hound stopping on the way so she could say bye to her mom and the boy's. On the way to the Gray Hound station Jan told Jesus and Dominique to take care of Marvaleen for her. Don't let her worry too much and don't let her do any heavy lifting and don't let her wear those tight shoe's any more. When you get home look under the bed and give her the new one's I bought for her.

Living It Up- Ann Jennings

At the bus station she hugged Jesus and told him she would see him for Christmas and gave Dominique a long kiss and told him she loved him. Dominique walked her to the bus and stayed there until the bus pulled away, thinking about his mom again. When the bus turned the corner he walked back to the car where Jesus was waiting to take him home. For the next four week's Jan studied hard, aced three tests and got an 80 on two. A card arrived three week's later announcing baby JJ and a picture. She couldn't wait to get home to hold him. It had been day's since she seen Sophy, they would always just miss each other. Jan was looking forward to the Christmas break just to clear her head. Rose a girl from down the hall was driving home to Wisconsin and asked Jan if she wanted a ride home and Jan jumped on the invitation.

Living It Up- Ann Jennings

I love your name Jan told Rose are you named after the flower? No actually I'm named after my mom Rose said her name is Rosie Ann and she went here about a hundred years ago and she wanted me to go to the same school she went to. Jan laughed at the expression on Jan's face when Rose told her about her mom is that where you got that long thick red pony tail too Jan asked? "Yep" Rose said and what about the freckles Jan said who did you get them from? Another gift from my mom Rose said. What about your dad Jan asked? Never knew the man Rose said, him and my mom met here in college fell in love my mom got pregnant with me then they separated and when I was two he died on his motor cycle that's all I know, so did he even know about you Jan asked "nope" Rose said.

I asked my mom his name when I got older and found his picture while snooping through my mom's room one day and saw that he was very handsome and had the cutest little nose. This time Jan would have two weeks at home she helped Rose on the gas as far as Chicago. She told Rose to come in and meet her mom and rest up before heading back out for the last hour and forty five minutes to Wisconsin. Jan thought when she got home she would help her mom decorate the tree, but when Rose turned the corner the house was all decorate with light's and a big wreath on the door and through the window was the prettiest tree she had ever seen.

Her friend Rose said "Damn girl yo mom sure know how to decorate." Which Jan found out later Dominique did most of the work. Christmas break went the same as Thanksgiving but only this time baby JJ joined them. Baby JJ was the most beautiful baby Jan had ever seen, she held him while he slept and hummed him a lullaby. Everyone went to church Christmas morning and Rev. Taylor christened JJ after church they all went back to the Peters house for a big breakfast which the two moms prepared.

Living It Up- Ann Jennings

After breakfast they all opened presents and Jan was pleased that everyone loved their gift from her. Her dad even called and said he liked the insect book she had mailed to him. He had always been interested in insects. When Jan was little he would take her to the park and instead of playing in the playground her and her dad would collect insect's and put them in a jar. After they opened all the present's the girl's move to the kitchen to start Christmas dinner leaving the guy's to clean up all the wrapping all over the living room floor.

 The turkey was in the sink ready to be seasoned and stuffed. Mrs. Peters told Jan to get the big bowl from under the cabinet and crumble the corn bread up in it, and Marv you get the cans of chicken broth out of the top cabinet and open them, and then she started chopping up onions and celery. Mrs. Peters told Marvaleen add the broth to Jan's bowl then she added her onions and celery and seasoning. The girl's sang while they cooked and played Christmas music. Jan put the turkey in the roaster pan and Mrs. Peters told Marvaleen what seasoning's to get out the cabinet and she seasoned the turkey then Jan stuffed the dressing into the turkey and it was ready for the oven. Wow let's start on our deserts Mrs. Peters said, you will need another bowl, I'll get it Jan said ok you get the mixer she said to Marv in that cabinet she said pointing.

Ok now we will need six cups of this cake flour sifted she told them, I'll do the first one to show you how. They took turns sifting until they had six cup's, now we will need to crack six egg's, I'll do it Marv said, "I know how to do that" ok you get the butter out Jan's mom said and Ill measure the three cups of sugar, now all we need is vanilla, Marv got the vanilla out the seasoning cabinet. Jan turned the mixer on to beat the batter while Marvaleen oiled the pound cake pan. Jan poured the cake batter into the pan and put it in the 350 degree second oven. Marvaleen said I always wondered why there were two ovens on your stove now I see why.

Now on to the vegetables Mrs. Peters said, she showed the girl's how to make spinach sulfa, glazed carrots, potato salad homemade cranberry sauce and homemade eggnog. These are my grandmother's recipes she told them. Rose called to wish them a Merry Christmas then Jan had an idea and told her to come a day early so she can get a good night's sleep there before they headed out Rose thought that to be a good idea. After they finished the delicious meal Mrs. Peters asked who wanted more sweet potato pie? They all moaned. You kid's go have fun, the boy's and I will clean up here, are you sure mom Jan said? Yes that would give us something to do right boys? They all shook their heads. The five of them left and went back to Marvaleen and Jesus apartment. After putting baby JJ to bed the four of them played music and danced until after two.

Living It Up- Ann Jennings

The next morning Jesus offered to drive them home but Jan said they would take the bus. But it's cold outside Marvaleen said they're in love Jesus said, "Oh" was all Marvaleen could say. When Rose came back through Chicago to pick up Jan she slept in Jan's room and the next morning Mrs. Peters fixed a big breakfast before they left. Jan wasn't ready to go because after she went back this time it would be four months before she would be back, for summer break and then she would be starting her sophomore year. Marvaleen and her mom agreed to visit at different times.

To her surprise Dominique came to visit in February on Valentine's Day. He told Jan he took the bus but actually he hitch hiked all the way telling the driver's that picked him up that he was a college student trying to get back to school. The two day's and one night he was there they sat down stairs in the sitting room of Jan's dorm. The next month on March fifteenth Marvaleen came to see her and got a cheap motel room for two day's she went to class with Jan and sat in the back of the class room. Jan took her friend to dinner and they talked into the night in Marvaleen's motel room.

Living It Up- Ann Jennings

At the beginning of April Mrs. Peters and the boys came after she got the ok that she can take them to another State Jan the boy's and her mom had fun shopping and went to a movie one night and Jan introduced them to her professors. Jan was sad when they left but she knew she would see them again in one month. When Ms. Peters and the boys returned home she had a message from the agency to give them a call when she called the agency it was just as she predicted only nine months with the boys and now the grandmother wanted them back it was hard seeing them leave.

On May third the last day of school Jan was expecting her mom to pick her up with all her bags "they had to take all their belongings because they may not have the same room next year" but to her surprise Dominique came in a dinted up van, where did you get this Jan said. It's my dad's; I told him I need to borrow it for a couple of days. You never mentioned your dad to me before Jan said, and I didn't know you even had a driver's license. I had to show it to your mom before she would let me come to get you I got it two months ago.

Living It Up- Ann Jennings

On the ride home Jan asked Dominique, will I get to meet your dad. He manages the gas station on Beaver Run Road, he work's sixteen hours a day, and we live with his mom who's always high. Oh I'm so sorry Jan said; don't be... Dominique said, I'm use to it I've been living with them since grade school ever since my mom left us. I also have five step brothers. I always see one of my brother's Lawrence but I don't let him see me I understand Jan said would you like for me to go with you to visit them?

I'm not ready yet Dominique said. Where's your mom Jan asked she said she couldn't take it any more Dominique said and left us, I see her on TV and in the paper a lot. Is your mom famous Jan asked no she's not she's the mistress of a millionaire. Is this millionaire married Jan asked, yes Alexander Garrett You mean tall overly handsome blue eyes blond hair very successful Alexander Garrett the famous movie producer Jan said. That's him Dominique said and my mom don't care.

Apparently his wife don't care either Jan said.
After the long drive home Jan had learned
everything she always wanted to know about
Dominique's family. The following week Jan,
Dominique, Marvaleen and Jesus went to Las
Vegas for four days leaving baby JJ with
Marvaleen's parents. Her parents were very
poor but Marvaleen took everything baby JJ
would need for the four days and her parents
didn't have to spend a penny on buying him
anything.

Jan's mom dropped the four of them off at the
airport Thursday afternoon at twelve noon. On
the plane ride everyone was too excited to
rest. When the plane flew over Vegas and
they saw all the light's their eye's got big as
saucers. "Wow" they all said in unison. At the
airport a van from the Treasure Island hotel
was waiting for them to take them to the hotel.
When they got to the TI hotel they went up to
room. This is beautiful Marvaleen said, the
room had two king size bed's and a small
fridge and microwave. Jan and I will take this
bed Marvaleen said putting her bag on the bed
closest to the bathroom and you and
Dominique can have that one she said to her
husband.

Living It Up- Ann Jennings

Come look at this view Dominique said looking out the big eighth floor picture window. "Wow" they all said, hey there's a Burger King Dominique said pointing across the street. Whose hungry Jan said? After they finished unpacking they walked to Burger King and ate burger's and coke. Well are we ready to play the machine's Jesus said, he had brought sixty dollar's for him and Marvaleen to play on the machine's, Dominique had got thirty dollar's from his dad to play on the machine's and the air fare and money for food, Jan's mom had gave her one hundred dollars to play with. After they finished eating they walked back across the street and went for a walk through all the hotels.

That night they saw a parrot show outside the TI then walked across the street and watched the people in the gondola in front of the Vanessa Hotel. Then they walked back across the street to their hotel and played the machines. Jesus put a five dollar bill in the Haywire Machine and on the eighth pull won fifty dollar's and decided to quit for the night while he was ahead. Maravleen won eleven on her second pull on the quarter machine, Dominique lost fifteen dollar's in three minutes, Jan put twenty dollar's in her machine and lost it in two minutes, they decided they had played enough for the night.

Back up in the room the boy's decided to take their shower before they went to bed so the girls could have the bathroom in the orning. Hey there's a second TV in here Dominique said from the bathroom. After the boy's showered and got into bed the girl's got into their bed and they all talked for another three hours before they all fell asleep. The next morning when Jan woke Marvaleen was already getting out the shower and the boys were still sleep in the next bed. Marvaleen came out the bathroom and told Jan she could take her shower.

Jan got up collected her things and went into the bathroom, when she came out fully dressed Marvaleen was talking quietly to Jesus. He decided to get dressed next since Dominique was still sleep, when Jesus finished in the bathroom Dominique was woke and collecting his clothes to wear for the day After Dominique came out dressed they all went down to have a continental breakfast in the hotel. After a big hearty breakfast they walked to the other end of the strip to the beautiful Mandalay Hotel in the old Vegas and took the double Decker bus called the Duce back. When they got off the Duce in front of their hotel there was a crowd of people gathered around they went to see what they were doing.

Living It Up- Ann Jennings

A man was selling tickets to David Coper field's magic show the tickets were forty five dollar's each more than what they wanted to pay. Well how about Diana Ross ticket's for ten dollar's the man said. Let me pay Jan said giving the man forty dollar's and collecting the four ticket's. After entering they found out they had front roll seats. When Diana Ross came on stage Jan said "she's beautiful." Diana Ross sang a lot of song's they didn't know and on the one's they knew they got up and danced in front of the stage. After two and a half hours they walked out happy to have found a concert for only ten dollar's.

Then TI was showing the Parrot show again and they watched it for the second time, then walked back inside and played the machines again. Jesus played ten dollar's before he won three hundred dollar's then he decided he was done, Dominique played two dollar's before he won forty dollar's, Marvaleen played five dollar's before she won forty five dollars, Jan played twenty dollar's and lost it all, then put in another dollar and won seventy dollar's. They walked back across the street to Burger King for dinner. After Burger's and coke again they walked back to their hotel and went up to their room.

The boy's took their shower again and they all got into their pajamas and watched TV and talked until after midnight. The next morning was just like the first Marvaleen woke at seven thirty as she did every morning at home because that's what time JJ woke up. She showered then Jan got up and showered then the boy's went last. After a big breakfast down stairs they walked to the other end of the strip again and shopped at some of the stores on the strip they decided to walk back this time. They saw a sign saying one dollar foot long hotdog and decided to have one for lunch. The little restaurant was about the size of a bedroom and very crowded.

They ordered their hotdog and one large order of fries to share, after they finished their lunch they walked back to their hotel. Outside their hotel a girl was passing out ticket's announcing a dance tonight, they decided that they should go. They went up to their room the boy's got dressed first and left the room and went down stairs and told the girl's when they get ready to just come down. Marv and Jan got all dressed up and Marv let Jan try her lipstick and Jan let Marv use the new perfume she had just bought that day. They left their room at nine and met the boy's in the lobby; "wow" you two look nice Dominique said. They made their way down the hall and a room was set up with a déjà, refreshments, and a dance floor with lights under the floor. They got a table and Jan dragged Dominique to the dance floor.

After eating the refreshment's and dancing till three in the morning they went back up to their room where they decide to pack their suit case's before they went to bed. They only had four hours before they would leave for the airport. After they finished packing and taking their shower it was four in the morning, we'll let's get three hours of sleep Marv said. The next morning they took their suitcase's down with them to breakfast. After breakfast the hotel van took them back to the airport. We didn't get to play the machine's Jesus said, they have them at the airport the driver said, will we get there in time to play before our flight Jesus said? Yes you have plenty of time he told him.

After they checked in and got their boarding passes they walked to the gate and found a roll of machines just like the driver said they each got on a machine and they all got lucky. Jesus hit for five hundred on his fourth pull-on the machine, Marv hit for four hundred, Dominique hit for three hundred and Jan hit for one hundred. They collected their winnings, got on their plane and fell asleep. Jan's mom was waiting for them at the airport when they returned. She stopped at Marvaleen's parent's to get the baby then dropped them off at home then she dropped Dominique off and on their way home Jan told her mom all the fun they had. Jan's mom was so happy to see her daughter happy because she knew how hard she worked at school and when she goes back to school this time she would be more relaxed.

The four day's went fast but they had to leave so Jesus could go back to work. The rest of Jan's summer went by with movies, picnic, babysitting, parties' and something Jan had always wanted to do, sky dive. Jan was still on cloud nine when she went back to start her junior year. That year Jan didn't come home on the holiday's, she stayed at school and volunteered at one of the biggest Vet hospital's in Georgia Dominique came once to visit her. But nothing could stop her from going home on her mother's birthday. On the morning of Mrs. Peter's birthday the agency called and told her that the three boys that came to her house earlier that year was living with their grandparents but now she says she can't handle them she says the boy's argue too much among themselves so I'm calling to see if you would like to foster them before the lady could get all the words out this Peters was asking her when will they be here?

I'm going to pick them up now I could bring them right over. Mrs. Peters rushed to get the two bedrooms ready for the boys she was hoping to call her own. She was so excited I think this time it will work she said to herself. After cleaning the rooms for the boys she decides to call Jan. When the agency returned with the boys they were happy to see Ms. Peters. Percy made grandma cry Parnell said. You shut up Perry said then all three boys started to argue among themselves. The agent started to speak when Mrs. Peters said in a stern voice "That kind of action among you brothers stops right now" all three boys stood there with their mouths open.

The agent told Ms. Peters that she would leave and let her have a talk with the boys and if she needed her to just call. Oh I think we will be just fine right boys? Yes ma'am they all said in unison Ms. Peters enrolled the boys back in the same school they were in when they were there before. The boys were given three dollars a week and every time they would argue they would have to put a quarter in the jar on this Peter dresser then at the end of the month Mrs. Peters would double what the boy's had. Jan was only there for two days and had to rush back to take a finial in biology class that she couldn't miss. It didn't matter that Dominique had only came to see her once that school year they still talked on the phone every night at nine sharp and they were still madly in love this was something either one of them could shake. The rest of her junior year flew by.

Living It Up- Ann Jennings

Sophy graduated and Jan bought her a one way plane ticket home. Roes offered Jan a ride home again that summer and Dominique asked if he could meet them half way and ride back with them Rose agreed, Jan had told her all about Dominique. He met the girl's in Myrtle Beach borrowing his dad's cell phone to stay in touch with them. Rose told her that her roommate graduated and she would love for Jan to be her roommate the next school year my roommate Sophy graduated also Jan told her. Both girls' thought that was a good idea and Jan decided to move into Rose room because it was closer to the bathroom. Both girls' sang to the radio for the rest of the ride to Myrtle Beach where they picked up Dominique at a truck stop where he hitch hiked a ride to.

Rose saw that they loved each other more than life. Jan had a wonderful summer at home and so did Rose in Wisconsin. Three days before school started back Rose came and spent the night at Jan's before the long drive back. Jan was happy the boy's came back. Jan's senior year was even harder but her mind stayed focus when it wasn't on Dominique. Then at the beginning of her senior year everything changed. Her father came to visit her with a lady at his side he introduced as his fiancée' and holding the lady's hand was a young girl about three with big brown eyes and curly hair and looked like her from the picture's she seen of herself when she was three. She was lost for words but also happy for them.

You always wanted a baby sister well meet Maxine and you and Maxine will be having another baby sister in about six months. They all went out to dinner and Jan was surprised that she actually liked the lady and her sister. In less than a year Jan had gained three step brothers, one step sister and another step sister on the way. She couldn't wait until nine to tell Dominique. The rest of her senior year went well, and her graduation was in two days. She would still have three more years of schooling on site at the hospital before becoming a Veterinarian. Saturday morning she went to get her hair and nails done, then at noon she had graduation practice. She was hoping to see Dominique but she was too busy packing up her room.

Everyone showed up to the graduation, Dominique, Marv, baby JJ, Jesus, her mom and her three new brothers, her dad and his new wife, and her step sister Maxine. After graduation they all went to dinner. She had four months before she had to report to the Veterinarian hospital in New Orleans to do one year volunteer and get graded. When they got back to Chicago she and Dominique spent every waking moment together. She moved into the apartment over the garage so the boys could each have their own room inside the house. The year in New Orleans was harder than Jan ever suspected, she talked to Dominique every night that year at nine and stayed up most nights after she talked to him studying. She worked on every animal from a hamster to a horse.

She knew her mom and Dominique were coming to her award ceremony but she was surprised to see Rose came also. After the award ceremony they all went back to Chicago and Jan's mom surprised her with a new car parked inside the garage. Rose stayed with Jan in her apartment over the garage for one night before going home. Jan took her brother's skating and bowling, to the movies and to the park swimming pool they loved Dominique. Her last two years would be in Illinois at the Emergency Vet Hospital. During the next two years after Dominique left her house every night at nine she would stay up to midnight studying. The two years really drained her, she was so tired. She told her mom after graduation she would take six months off before going to work and her mom agreed with her saying she should go on a vacation.

Two weeks before graduation Dominique came to see her and that night when he got ready to leave he told her he was going down to Florida with three friends but he would be back before her graduation. You better Jan said, I won't walk across that stage until you get there. The day of the graduation was hectic for Jan, she didn't get to see anyone, but she knew everyone was there. When they called her name Dr. Jan Peters she walked across the stage proudly to receive her license the last piece of the puzzle.

Living It Up- Ann Jennings

After the ceremony she still hadn't seen any of her family until she walked into the lobby and seen all her family there waiting for her. After all the hugs she said where's Dominique? Did he go to the men's room? Everyone's face changed then everyone started walking away leaving Marvaleen, Jan's mom and dad. What's wrong Jan said? Why are you all looking at me like that? They all looked at each other but Marvaleen was the first to talk he's gone Jan. I know that but where? Then her dad said he's gone for good honey. What do you mean Jan said. Let's go to the car and I'll explain her mom said. "NO" explain what? Where's Dominique? With tears in her eyes her mom said his father came over last week to tell us Dominique was stabbed in the Florida Airport and he's gone honey. Jan didn't remember anything after that.

When she woke the paramedics was giving her oxygen. She looked at her mom and asked what happened. After the paramedics released her they got into her mom's car and on the way home her mom told her she wanted to be alone with her before they got home. Mrs. Peters told Jan Dominique went to Florida with some old friends that he used to hang out with and when they got there they took him to some friends of theirs that deal in drugs. The guy's knew Dominique didn't work and asked him would he like to make five thousand dollars. Dominique looked at his friends he came down with and they told him it was up to him.

Dominique never had a job and couldn't turn that kind of money down so he decided to do what they wanted. They gave him a suit case and gave him an address and told him to deliver the suit case and bring back the money. Dominique's three friends said they would stay there until he came back. He took a cab to the address and delivered the suitcase and made the exchange. They opened the suitcase to see the drugs then opened the suitcase and showed Dominique the money. Dominique had never seen so much money in his life. He let out a long whistle and asked "man how much money is this?" Fifty thousand, that was the deal right? Dominique said "oh yea" that's right.

After he walked out, at that moment he
decided he wasn't going back. He hailed a cab
and went straight to the airport and purchased
a ticket to Chicago from the money in the suit
case. The guy's that gave him the suit case
were getting nervous and called to see where
Dominique was. The guy's told him the drop
was made forty five minutes ago. He told his
accomplish "let's go" they went to the airport
and found Dominique walking toward the
plane. They walked behind Dominique, stabbed
him in the back, took the case, and kelp
walking. This happened last week we didn't tell
you last week because we knew you would not
have gone through with your graduation.

Dominique's father agreed with us. His funeral was this morning, I'm so sorry honey her mom said crying. Jan wanted to know where he was buried and when they got home Jan didn't go up to her apartment she got in her car and went to Dominique's grave. She cried until she had no more tears. The next morning her mother noticed her car wasn't there so she called Marvaleen's house looking for her. She's not here Marvaleen told her, her and Jesus went to the grave yard and Jan was still there from the day before they drove her home and Marvaleen and Mrs. Peters put her to bed. For the next three weeks Jan was at Dominique's grave every day all day. Her mom told her it wasn't healthy so Jan decided to take a day off and stayed in bed. Her mom brought her chicken soup, she got up at six p.m. took a shower, ate her soup and went back to bed crying herself to sleep.

In her dream that night she opened her eyes and Dominique was sitting on the side of her bed looking at her, she jumped up and grabbed him and they lay in her bed holding each other but when she woke the next morning he was gone. Jan turned the light off in her bathroom and walked the four steps to her bed. She hugged her pillow and started to cry. In her dream an arm came around her and Dominique said don't cry Jan I'm here. Jan jumped; don't be scared I'm sorry I left you. Jan looked at Dominique and said is it really you? Yes it's me Dominique said but if I scared you I'll go away. No I want you to stay Jan said, okay then I'll stay.

Dominique explains to her what had happened and it was the same story her mother had told her. Jan fell asleep in Dominique's arms and the next morning Dominique was gone again. The next morning Jan was in a good mood, she went to return her mom's bowl and told her that the soup was good. Her mom and brothers were glad to see her in a good mood and a smile on her face. It had been a week since they saw her smile. Jan told her mom about her dream. She stayed late that night watching TV with her mom and brothers she walked through the yard and up the stairs to her garage apartment.

Living It Up- Ann Jennings

Without turning on any lights she went to run a bubble bath. She soaked for 45 minutes thinking of Dominique after her bath she walked to her bedroom turned the light on just to see if he was there but he was not. She slipped into bed still thinking about him and fell asleep. She felt his arm slipping around her, I missed you today Jan told Dominique, she told him she watched TV with her brothers and read to them as Dominique listened to her he was rubbing his hands over her nude body until he hit a sensitive spot that sent chills through Jan's body. They make passionate love to each other than Jan fell asleep.

 In the morning when she woke Dominique was gone. Jan was glad the day passed quickly she wanted to ask Dominique why he's never here when she wakes. Her mom called her at 8:10 that night as Jan was getting out the tub to see if she wanted to play checkers, Jan said she was tired and was getting ready for bed. But it's only eight her mom said I know Jan said but remember we were up late last night ok her good night her mom said but come for breakfast.

Jan couldn't wait to turn off the lights and slip into bed. When she fell asleep Dominique came right on schedule she forgot about the question she wanted to ask him and went straight to kissing him. Their lovemaking was magical nothing like they ever imagine and again the next morning he was gone. The next night when he came Jan was sitting up in her bed not realizing she had fallen asleep and eating ice and asked Dominique if you would like some, no I don't eat he why not? Jan asked? I don't know I'm never hungry Dominique said.

Why can't I see you in the day time Jan asked? I don't know Dominique said when you dream that's my sigh to come to you. Jan started visiting Marvaleen again and playing with her now two godchildren. JJ wanted a little sister but got a little brother instead and said okay I guess I'll keep him. Jan also went to Florida to visit her dad when her stepsister was born and to New Orleans to visit Rose. Jan asked Dominique one night where do go during the day? I don't know Dominique said I only know when I come here maybe I'm sleep somewhere.

Living It Up- Ann Jennings

Their love for each other was the kind of love one can't even imagine. It can't even be entered into one's mind it was just that powerful Jan compared their love to that of God and his Son. One night when Dominique came to Jan's bed in her dream he didn't look happy. What's wrong Jan asked? I have to leave Dominique said my time is up. What do you mean? You can't leave Jan said.

This will be our last night together Jan; No I won't let you go Jan cried and held him tight. You can't keep me here he said I have stayed as long as I can you have to get on with your life there innocent animals out there that need you to make them well, it's time for you to go do what you always wanted to do. Go be that great emergency Vet surgeon and make your parents proud. No Jan said I want to go with you. You can't I'm sorry Dominique said Jan was crying uncontrollable now I'll hold you until you fall asleep. I'm not going to sleep she said in her dream and held him tight still crying.

At 6 AM she was still holding him tight and crying begging to go with him and when she closed her eyes for three seconds and opened them he was gone. Only three days after her son's funeral Alexander told Tori it was time for her to come back home. Leigh Kay and Tori's brother Ronald didn't like the way Tori let Alexander rule her like she was his slave. Even though he showed her the finer things in life something they knew Tori always wanted and she lived like a princess with him controlling her every move. Leigh Kay had even read in some magazine that he beat her up one time sending her to the emergency room. But she still loved that fast life style and no one could talk her into coming back home.

Even if she did Mr. Garrett would probably hunt her down and have her killed Leigh Kay said. In the thirty years they were together Alexander had bought her an island in Trinidad, took her on a month's cruse for the entire month of her birthday. He flew her to Spain in his private jet and when they landed in an empty field with beautiful flowers, a table was there set up with candles, caviar, and champagne chilling on ice this is beautiful Tori said, happy birthday Alexander said. He took her skiing in the French Alps, on a European tour. He rented out an entire mall and let Tori go on a shopping spree, all the stores catered to her and all the restaurants stood in front of the restaurant holding trays of food for her to taste when she passed.

When he had to go to Sidney he called Tori and told her to pack her bags he would pick her up in a hour for Australia, this was something Tori had got used to that's why she had to always keep her hair done. Dominique's brothers, Ronald, Eugene, Lawrence and Richard cried at their brother's casket Mickey only cried because he seen his brother's crying, Sheeree his grandmother came up and took his hand and lead him back to his seat.

Cindy came with her new husband Christopher and couldn't hold back her tears even though she tried to be strong for Thomas and her daughter. Dominique's dad and his mom Gloria had to be escorted out the funeral home for making a scene. Marvaleen chose not to go to the funeral that morning knowing it would show on her face when she went to Jan's graduation that same day, but Jesus said he had to go. Leigh Kay said she had to fly back after the graduation she was on call in the emergency room the next day.

Since high school Lawrence told his brother Richard what he expected of him and what he didn't like. Every time Richard would bring home a girl his brother Lawrence would have to approve of her and if he didn't Richard was not allowed to see her again. If Richard wanted to wear a certain outfit to school and his brother Lawrence didn't like it Lawrence would make him change. Their grandmother Sheeree would tell Lawrence to be easy on Richard. In high school Richard finally started taking back his life, and being very resentful toward his brother. Lawrence had turned all of Richard's girlfriends away until Richard's last year in college when he brought home Paris.

Living It Up- Ann Jennings

Paris was five eight one hundred and eight pounds with long blond hair and white creamy skin. Paris sister London was crazy about Richard ever since Paris brought him to her sister's house during Spring break from college. But when Paris took him to her parent's house for Thanksgiving the atmosphere wasn't as comfortable. One year later Richard and Paris graduated and became successful lawyers. A year after that they got married with everyone's blessing except Paris mother. After three years of marriage Richard Jr. was born, the next year Byron was born and then two years later Benjamin came alone three handsome curly hair sons "which their grandpa Thomas thinks all look just like him." They decided to give up their 14th floor condo in down town Chicago with the breath taking view to have a house built in Georgia.

When they moved to Georgia they had to get use to the stares from people all over again. Then after five years of marriage Paris mom was finally coming around to liking Richard. After college Lawrence became a successful CEO buying major companies that were failing, putting the money into them to save them then owning half the company. As CEO Lawrence immediate and absolute obedience from his mimesis no matter what he asked he was an astute business man and had an enormous amount of charm. He underwent a totally complete format from child to young adult to running for mayor in just months. He moved much faster than his brothers even the older ones Lawrence applied principle and theories without regard for practical difficulties or individual circumstances.

Living It Up- Ann Jennings

Lawrence meet Lindsey Renee when she was hired at one of his company's as a receptionist when Mrs. Jones had to leave because her husband's job was moving to Detroit. When Lawrence dropped by one day Lindsey Renee took one look at him and knew she had to have him. The next time he returned to the company she was working she wore the shortest and tightest skirt in her closet and invited Lawrence to lunch. After they had lunch Lindsey Renee told Lawrence that she was still living at home and was looking for her own place. He told her he lived in a condo and the one across the street was empty and gave her the address. When Lindsey Renee got off work she went to enquire about the condo. The owners met her there and told her she would need first and last month's rent.

Lindsey Renee wrote the check right there and the owner gave her the keys. The condo had high ceilings and floor to floor windows, one bed room, kitchen with a deck, a living room and two baths. Lindsey Renee was so excited when she got home she told her parents she was moving. She gave her mom a spare key and the address to her new condo and told her she could go see the place while she was at work the next day. And she would be moving out the week end. Lindsey Renee called Helen her best friend and told her to meet her at the Dress Barn at five; she needed to go shopping for new clothes.

Living It Up- Ann Jennings

So what do you think? Lindsey Renee asked
Helen as she modeled the black dress in the
mirror. Lindsey Renee knew Helen wouldn't
bite her tongue and would tell her the truth.
He's cute Helen said, but you're wasting your
time, the guy doesn't even know you're alive.
But you should see the way he looks at me
when I walk by Lindsey Renee said in a singing
voice, no thanks Helen said. Then Lindsey
Renee started to cry, why don't he like me?
Helen hurried to her side and put her arm
around her friend. Come on Lindsey Renee he's
not worth it, why do you do this to yourself
every time. Sure Lawrence is cute but he
doesn't want you. He's definitely a looker, I
could even go for him myself, but I've seen his
kind before. Smooth talker, handsome as all
outdoors, definitely a ladies' man, owns his
own businesses, expensive cars and a condo
down town and he's running for major.

Living It Up- Ann Jennings

Helen told her friend I hate to see you crying your eyes out over a total stranger. "He's not a stranger" Lindsey Renee said in a hostile voice we went to lunch and he told me all about himself. Not everything Helen said. The relationship was unbalanced; Lindsey Renee was perfectly monogamous while Lawrence had other women in his life. Do you want to see my place Lindsey Renee asked Helen? It's not furnished but I'll get my parents to do that for me. Helen helped Lindsey Renee carry her bags into her condo Helen looked around the condo and liked everything she saw can you afford this Helen asked. Well for a few months until I get what I want Lindsey Renee said. Do you want to help me move in this week end and spend the night Lindsey Renee said? I don't know Helen said I was gone last week end with you and my parent says they never see me.

Living It Up- Ann Jennings

Maybe I'll stay home this weekend and spend a little time with them. I only get to see them in the morning on my way out to work and in the evening I'm always with you and when I come home they're gone to bed. When Richard and Paris boys turned 6, 7, and 8, a five star hotel went bankrupt and they jumped on it and bought it. The hotel had six floors, twelve rooms on each floor. The lobby was breath taking, it included a full size gym, two swimming pools in and out, a pool room, a five star restaurant, a library, barber and beauty shop, massage parlor, nail shop a library, a night club, and a Kid's Tower catering to kid's of all ages. Four elevators but the fourth one only goes to the pen house that's rented out to only the rich. Richard had surveillance cameras put around the grounds of the hotel and on every floor. Lawrence heard about the hotel and wanted to buy it also he heard that his brother had already bought it he called Richard furious and told him he had to sell it to him.

Living It Up- Ann Jennings

After arguing with his brother for an hour Richard finally had to hang up on him. Two years later the brother's still was not speaking. Thomas tried his best to get Lawrence to call his brother but he was very defiant to his father. Thomas, Mickey and Sheeree moved into the guest house out back because the stairs was bothering Sheeree's knees. Eugene and Ronald called their father every week, but the only time he heard from Lawrence he tried to get his dad to talk to Richard and tell him to sell him the hotel.

Lindsey Renee and Lawrence had been seeing each other for two years; her mom would go to the grocery store every two weeks and fill up Lindsey Renee's refrigerator. She had not seen Lawrence for two weeks; she left him little meals outside his door and notes asking him to please call her. She called Helen and asked her to come over she had something big to show her. "Oh No" Helen said every time you say that I always wish I would have never seen it. But you got to see this Lindsey Renee said and you have to wait until tonight. "Oh no now I know I don't want to see it Helen said." After spending all day with her parent's Helen packed her tooth brush and pajamas and drove down town to Lindsey Renee's.

On the ride down she wondered what big thing Lindsey Renee had to show her. She also thought she really need to spend more time with her parents, she sort of miss them lately Lindsey Renee dominated all of her time. When Helen got there Lindsey Renee told her it was not dark enough outside yet to show her the surprise. And suggest they do each other's hair and nails. Then at eight Lindsey Renee pulled a telescope out of her closet and put it on a pole set up in front of her bed room window facing Lawrence window.

"Lindsey Renee no" this is carrying it too far. What are you doing? You can get arrested for invasion someone's privacy, I think he's seeing someone else Lindsey Renee said how do you know that Helen asked? And how many dishes have you taken over to him. That's the point Lindsey Renee replied now I get to go over and collect all my casserole dishes back. Richard and Paris decided to give the hotel their last name, The Middleton had its grand opening seven months later. Lawrence was furious when he saw his brother and wife on the news announcing the opening of their hotel. Unlike his brothers and dad who was celebrating. The next week after the opening Paris got a call from London saying that their dad had passed away.

Living It Up- Ann Jennings

After the funeral Paris offered her mom a room in the hotel. Each room had a kitchenette with a small refrigerator with a freezer, micro wave, sink, separate bed room with a king size bed and a huge closet and flat screen TV, a living room with a big picture window a flat screen TV' and a bath room with a jetted tub and separate shower. Jackie, Paris mom was glad to give up the big house that her and her husband shared for twenty five years. She had been putting Paris in beauty pageants since she was three years old. There was a room in the house full of her trophies and tiaras in a glass case.

The beauty pageants was something Paris did for her mother it wasn't her passion but she wanted to please her mother and she saw the glow in her mom's eyes when she was running for the crown. And when she won the look on her mother's face was elated, something Paris always looked forward to seeing. Jackie even bought frames and put Paris out fits she wore in them and put them on the walls in the passion room as she called it. She had them lined up on the walls according to Paris age starting at age three to twenty one.

Living It Up- Ann Jennings

At the age of twenty one Paris was glad that she had got too old for beauty pageants. That was the day her mother lost her spark, her shine and her drive. Paris and her dad noticed the change in Jackie. She never smiled any more never wanted to go out she had lost all her passion. Then Paris didn't make it any better when she would come home from college and go to her sister London's house and bringing home an African American schoolmate. London had moved out and got married right after high school.

John Miller a good friend of Lawrence asked Lawrence if he would go with him to his retirement party in Florida. Lawrence needed the break and jumped on the chance to get out of town. He had bought a small construction company three weeks earlier and they were doing a job in Florida and this would give him a chance to check on the progress. When Carolyn meets Lawrence at her retirement party they both reached for the dipper in the punch bowl at the same time.

When their finger's touched Carolyn felt a feeling she hadn't felt in a very long time snatching her hand back as if Lawrence hand was fire, she said you go first; no I'm sorry after you Lawrence said are you one of the retires? Yes I am Carolyn said, you look so young Lawrence said. Tell that to my body Carolyn said I'm fifty she said "Wow" are you sure? You don't look a day over forty Lawrence told her. Well thank you for the compliment. And by the way my name is Carolyn I know it's right there on your name tag.

Oh Carolyn said looking down at the oversized name tag stuck to her dress that was given to all the retirees when they came in. Lawrence noticed Carolyn feeling a little embarrassed, held out his hand, Lawrence Middleton he said. Who are you here with Carolyn asked? My best friend John Miller from the Chicago office Lawrence replied, I don't think I know him Carolyn said. Every year they give this big retirement party for all those retiring from the company. We have a plant in every state you know, Carolyn said. Well I'm glad it was here in Florida this year Lawrence said, and I got to meet you.

The pleasure is all mines Carolyn said. Are you retired she asked Lawrence. No I'm not that lucky. Carolyn was shocked to find out Lawrence was only thirty years old, and CEO to about ten businesses. Do you know the old Williams mansion on Lake Street Lawrence asked? Yes I love that place Carolyn said; when I was a little girl my mom was their cook. Right now they're having some work done to it. Yes I know Lawrence said my company is doing the work. Are you kidding me Carolyn said in surprise? What are they doing to it? We are adding a new wing. It's a lovely house Carolyn said yes it is a very nice place. Oh here's John now Lawrence said.

Carolyn notice an oversized man wearing a gray suit heading toward them with the same oversized name tag stuck to his suit jacket but only his said John. So here you are John said I should have known you were somewhere talking to a pretty lady. Lawrence introduced John to Carolyn and John asked her what plant she was retiring from. Right here in Florida Carolyn said with a big smile on her face happy she didn't have to travel. Well I'm from the Chicago Office John offered; you know they paid our way for the one's retiring that had to travel, wiping the smile off Carolyn's face. That must have cost them a pretty penny, Carolyn said. How long were you with the company John asked? Fifteen years; what about you? Twenty three and happy to give it up to go fishing!

That sounds nice Carolyn said, knowing she didn't like fishing, but not knowing what else to say. Then Lawrence cleared his throat. Oh, I think my glass is empty John said shaking the ice in his glass and moving away from the two it was nice meeting you. They fixed themselves pickles, shaved turkey, chips and punch, and found a small table at the back of the room. The only people Carolyn knew there were her supervisor and the Florida plant manager. She was the only one retiring from the Florida plant that year. And John was the only person Lawrence knew there, because they were best friends.

Living It Up- Ann Jennings

Carolyn learned from Lawrence when John asked him to accompany his to his retirement party, he was happy to abolish he had been under a lot of stress and needed to get away. They talked and nibbled at their food while half listing to the owner of the company on stage, saying what a wonderful job the retiree's had done to make the job easier for the one's following them. Then he started giving out awards Carolyn only half heard them call her name. What's your last name Lawrence asked her? Sinclair, Carolyn said. I think they're calling you. Carolyn turned around in her chair and saw the owner of the company holding up an envelope calling her name for the third time. I'm here she said as she made her way up to the front of the room and on the stage to accept her award.

The owner had a lot to say about Carolyn he thanked her for all her hard work and told everyone about Carolyn's role in helping the company and the employees realize that joining a union was beneficial to everyone. And all of you are familiar with our Logistics System; well Carolyn was the one who designed that to help us keep track of all our equipment. She's also responsible for the laundry service we use. It was her idea to buy the laundry company we were using and hire our own staff and keep the money in the company.

Living It Up- Ann Jennings

Everyone stood and gave Carolyn a big round of applause for all her achievements. Carolyn was given an envelope as she left the stage. Back at the table Lawrence was still standing and clapping for her congratulations he told her. John's name was called next he received an envelope and praise for all his hard work and staying with the company for twenty three years and becoming supervisor of fifty four workers. After John received his envelop her went to congratulate Carolyn. Wow young lady you've been busy he told her, I didn't know you were such an asset to the company. Let's see what we have here John said ripping open the envelope; Carolyn noticed she was still holding her's and ripped it open also.

Inside John's envelop was a check for twenty three thousand and inside Carolyn's was one for fifteen thousand. I guess they gave us a thousand for each year we worked she said. Yes this will be my down payment for my fishing boat john said so what are you going to do with yours he asked her? I don't know Carolyn said right now I'll just put it in the bank. Well you kid's have fun John said walking away from the table, I'm going to mingle. By the end of the evening Carolyn found out Lawrence had a twin brother "he didn't tell her about Mickey" and had a condo in three states and had companies all over the world.

Living It Up- Ann Jennings

The construction company Lawrence partially owned was restoring an old mansion in Florida and their next job would take them to another state. The company was doing well since Lawrence bought into it; they just had to pick a job off the list of demands they would never get around to doing all of them. When people hire them to do a job they had to accommodate them with a hotel and meals which went into the price of the job. The company had sixteen employees, sometimes the job didn't call for all sixteen skills the company kept it's prices low and that's why they had enough jobs to last them the next two years without scheduling any more The waiting list was long but people didn't mind.

Richard and Paris were out to dinner when Paris told him the news that they would be having another baby. Are you sure Richard asked excited? Did you see a doctor? What did he say? Slow down papa. Yes I went to the doctor and he says the baby and I are fine. Richard kissed his wife across the table and told her how happy he was. The waiter brought champagne and Richard only let Paris drink one glass and when they got home that night they slept in each other's arms. Kimberly Garrett received a call from the private investigator she hired to follow Alexander he asked her to meet him at the same place in one hour.

Living It Up- Ann Jennings

When Kimberly Garrett arrived at the Bar and Grill in a neighbor she wouldn't usually visit she was wearing a long blond wig, big sun glasses, and a plaid coat left by one of her maids. Kimberly sat at the same table as before away from the window and ordered coffee and told the waitress to make sure the cup was clean this time. When the PI arrived and sat next to her he slipped her a brown envelop would you like to be alone he asked. Yes Kimberly said and handed him an envelope with the money in it. They shook hands and the PI walked out leaving Kimberly with the information she paid for. She didn't feel comfortable in the Bar and Grill and decided to take the information to the library in her neighborhood before reading the contents.

On the way to the library she took off the blond wig exposing her short red hair and threw it out the window on the street. At the library she took off the coat and glasses and put them in her trunk. When she entered the library she went to the quiet room where the college students go to study for an upcoming test. She sat at a table and started reading. She had suspected her husband of cheating six years ago as she read she found out he had actually been cheating for almost thirty years according to the report.

Her name was Tori Middleton; she had heard that name before. Her husband had opened up a bank account for her, bought her a new house, a new car, she also had an unlimited credit card and went on all his business trips with him as she read on it showed Tori's age which was seventeen years younger than her husband and when she got to the pictures she saw that Tori was black.

That son of a bitch she said a little too loud and a couple of heads turned to look at her. The private investigator had provided her with all the times they were together, all the parties all the affairs all the trips and the main one that Kimberly wanted to go on, the trip to the white house that Alexander told her he only had one invitation. The list went on and on but Kimberly had read enough. When her husband came home two days later from a business trip Kimberly told him she would be going out of the states for a couple of weeks. Lawrence hated to leave Florida and Carolyn, they spent the next three days together visiting the construction site and Carolyn told him the history of the old mansion.

Living It Up- Ann Jennings

Then it was time for Lawrence to get back to leave he asked Carolyn to come with him, I can't just pack up and leave Florida Carolyn said, I have friends and family here and I'm in the middle of writing a book on my life. The places I've been the people I've meet and the things I would like to do before I die. You can write a book anywhere Lawrence said. The adoption finally went through and Cindy was awarded the three boys she had been raising since they were 7, 8 and 10, now Jan went from an only child to having three adopted brothers and two half-sisters from her dad.

For the last three years Dominique had been coming to Jan in her dreams then one night he told her that this would be his last night. Why Jan said where will you go? I don't know Dominique said Jan held him tight and cried, but when she woke the next morning Dominique was gone and she knew she would never see him again. She told Cindy one day she would like to move to Africa. Marvaleen's and Jesus were working and doing very well even making enough to help out their parents, and baby JJ was in school and the teacher couldn't say enough good things about him. Jan had started putting money away for his college. Leigh Kay was worried about her friend, when she talked to Tori last night she sounded as if she was crying.

Why don't you just come home Leigh Kay told her you don't sound happy anymore. I'm happy Tori said it's just Alexander is getting to demanding and I think he's seeing someone else. He's always in a bad mood when he stops by and he never spends the night anymore and I know he's not going home to his wife. Come to New York and visit for a couple of day Leigh Kay said. Kimberly checked into a cheap motel and planed her next step. She had a black long wig and brown contacts to cover her blue eyes and the black outfit from the secondhand store.

After going over everything once more she drove her rental car to the house and waited. After Lawrence returned from Florida Lindsey Renee started in on him. Where have you been? I missed you. I've been away on business Lawrence told her checking on another one of my businesses. Would you like to have dinner tonight she asked him, not tonight Lawrence said I'm exhausted. At one in the morning Lawrence heard a knock on the door and when he opened the door Lindsey Renee was standing there and dropped her coat and was wearing only her birthday suit. Get in here Lawrence told her and took her to his bed.

Living It Up- Ann Jennings

Two weeks later Lawrence had to go to Hong Kong to check on another one of his companies and asked Carolyn if she would like to meet him there. They enjoyed two weeks in Hong Kong then went back to Florida and spent two weeks in Carolyn's bed only getting up to answer the door for the food they ordered. When Lawrence returned to home Lindsey Renee was furious when Lawrence told her he was in love with Carolyn. Lindsey Renee decided to give up her condo and move back home. A small warehouse was closing in Florida and Lawrence offered to buy into the company but they didn't want to be partners with Lawrence knowing his past so Lawrence waited for it to go on the market and bought it and transformed it into a mansion for him and Carolyn to live in.

The people of Florida had a love hate relation for Lawrence knowing everything he did for them he was actually thinking only of himself. It took a year and two construction Companies working together to finish the work Carolyn packed her things and moved to the new house. The newspaper said it was the most beautiful transformation ever. When his dad and brothers heard about it they called to congratulate him. After moving into the mansion Carolyn gave expensive parties every weekend and meeting new friends.

Living It Up- Ann Jennings

Lawrence was busy at his office passing laws to better the State of Florida and the people, getting more jobs and getting companies to bring their business to the people of Florida. He did everything for the people just to try to get their vote as an elected representative. Lawrence was actively involved in Party Politics and was hoping to seek personal or partisan gain often by scheming and maneuvering. He was skilled in the administration of the government and believed he could effect change for the better.

Some of the problems that beset Lawrence were too great to be dealt with. Lawrence talked to his dad and asked him to open a branch of Capable Hands Insurance in Florida to give his people jobs but his dad told him he was getting ready to retire and was turning the company over to Tori if she wanted it. Lawrence had many enemies taking advantage of ordinary people and tax payers and made easy life harder. The plan he wrote up would cost the seniors thousands of dollars a year and the plan was so severely conservative that the members of his own party rejected it.

After little David turned one Paris and Richard
wanted to try once more for a daughter but
Paris told him this would be the last one.
Kimberly lay on the lounge chair by the pool
enjoying the sun at the Paris Hilton. A shadow
blocked her sun and she opened her eyes and
the waiter was standing there with a drink on
his tray with an umbrella stuck out and a slice
of pineapple and cherry on a plastic spear.
From the gentleman across the pool he said.
Kimberly lowered her sunglasses and looked
and gave the gentleman a smile. She took the
glass and raised it to him and he raised his
back to her then started his way over to her.

Marcus Lucas the third he introduced himself to
Kimberly. May I sit Marcus said, please do
Kimberly said. This is a beautiful hotel Marcus
said, I love it here Kimberly said, I try to visit
Paris at least once a year. Will your husband
be joining us Marcus asked? No not this time
Kimberly said he's back in the states. Tori
wanted to go to the Bahamas to visit her mom
then to New York to visit Leigh Kay but when
she told Alexander he told her violently she
couldn't go, and to go out and buy a nice black
dress and meet him at the usual place at 8:30.

Living It Up- Ann Jennings

Tori knew not to question Alexander so she would bring the subject up again at the restaurant over dinner. She decided not to go shopping and wear one of the many black dresses hanging in her closet. At four she went and got her hair and nails done, when she returned at seven forty five a strange car was parked down the street from her house. The driver had long black hair and dark sunglasses on. Alexander had always told her to be aware of her surroundings. She went into the house and got into the shower, while in the shower she thought she heard a noise downstairs.

She called out to Alexander but he didn't answer, when she finished her shower and dried off she went down stairs and Alexander was nowhere in sight but the front door was ajar and she could have sworn she closed it when she came in. She couldn't think about that right now she had to hurry, Alexander hated when she was late. No matter how hard they tried Paris could not get pregnant, her mom Jackie told her they should go on a vacation and leave the boys with her maybe that would relieve the stress. Richard didn't know what the problem could be they never had a problem before.

Maybe it was only meant for us to have the four boys Paris told him one night. I know how much you would like a daughter Richard told her she cried in her husband's arms until she fell asleep. Tori left the house at 8:00 looking like a million bucks, at the restaurant she handed her keys to the valet and went to the powder room before going to the table. In the powder room she put powder on her cheeks and nose to dull the shine. As she approached the table Alexander gave her a discussing look. Why did you wear that dress he asked her through clenched teeth? I like this dress Tori said, I told you to go out and buy a new one today I've already seen you in that one. Don't ever disobey me again Alexander said a little too loud and a few heads turned to look at them.

Living It Up- Ann Jennings

This is a ten thousand dollar dress Tori said, I don't care if it cost twenty thousand Alexander shouted at her I don't ever want to see you in the same dress twice, is that understood, he said squeezing her arm across the table. The waiter came over to their table and asked was everything ok, yes everything's fine and we're leaving Alexander said. Alexander took Tori's arm and escorted her out the restaurant. Outside he handed the valet both their tickets, while waiting for their cars he told Tori don't ever embarrassed me like that again, when I tell you to go buy a new dress that's what I mean, but you said you like this dress when I wore it to the White House Tori reminded him. And even the first lady thought it was exquisite. I loved it on you then but I wanted to see you in something different Alexander said, is that too hard for you to do Mrs. Spellman?

Now the people will talk saying you came to the restaurant wearing the same dress you wore to the white house. The valet brought their cars around and Alexander slipped him a tip. When the valet opened the door for Tori he noticed her holding her right arm and she gave him a little smile feeling a little embarrassed. Alexander told her to go straight home and he would be right behind her. She drove straight home as Alexander had told her, she thought he was going to come in but when she got there at nine thirty and entered the house Alexander sped off burning rubber.

Marcus and Kimberly had dinner that night and the next four nights until she told him she had to get back to her husband. Marcus hated to see her go but he had to get back to his wife also. They had one last drink in Kimberly's room that night and said their goodbyes. When Kimberly got home Alexander was in a bad mood, he snapped at her every word. When he left for the office Kimberly turned the TV on and seen the picture of Tori and the news announcer was saying still no answers to the murder of Tori Spellman.

Tori Spellman was found in her home last week and the police suspect her lover the well-known Alexander Garrett. Mr. Garrett is out on bail and the police are still looking for answers, if anyone knows anything about this case please call your local police department. When Thomas and the boys first heard the news they wanted her body shipped to Chicago. They wanted to give her a proper funeral and bury her next to her oldest son Dominique. Leigh Kay sat at the back of the church and cried in her mother's arms the whole service, she *couldn't* make herself go up and see her best friend in a coffin, she wanted to always remember her as she was the last time she saw her.

Living It Up- Ann Jennings

Cindy flew in from California and Dominique took the day off and came with his mom Gloria and she was sober. Jan read about it in the paper and came to give her condolences to Dominique's dad since she wasn't at his funeral; the funeral was small and simple. All the boys were there and Mickey even though he was in his thirty's still couldn't understand why everyone was crying. Kimberly turned off the TV and went to unpack and when she tried to go out that afternoon the media was in front of her house taking pictures and stuck a mike in her face "Do you think your husband killed his mistress?" "Did you know Mrs. Spellman?" "Will you stick by your husband?" Kimberly rushed to her car closed the door and drove off.

At dinner that evening the servants were very quiet, as usual Kimberly ate alone at their huge dining table and Alexander came in after midnight after Kimberly had already went to bed. The trial went on for three weeks and the verdict came back hung jury. Even though all the evidence pointed to Alexander, he was the last one seen with her and people say they saw them arguing at the restaurant and he grabbed her arm and stormed out. The valet said she was holding her arm when she got into her car, and a neighbor said when he left her house around nine thirty he was furious, she wanted to go check on her but was afraid he might come back.

After Alexander was acquitted he went back to work as if nothing happened. But he always wondered who would want to kill Tori, as far as he knew she had no enemies. Maybe he should have let her go to the Bahamas and New York that week. He cancelled her credit card and sold the house and called her friend Leigh Kay and told her to come and get what she wanted. Leigh Kay flew in from New York and cleaned out Tori's house taking her expensive paintings that Tori bought when she was there visiting her, her clothes and jewelry and her new car which she would give to one of the boys. She asked Alexander what she should do with the cloths because it was something she never wore. He suggests she sell them in an auction in New York.

Eight months after Tori's funeral Christopher called to inform them that Cindy had passed away in her sleep. He flew her body back to Chicago and they buried her next to her daughter and grandson this time Sheeree kelp Mickey at home. Then Christopher flew back to the Bahamas broken hearted. When Lawrence flew back to Florida from his mom's funeral the cleaning crew was at his house cleaning up from one of Carolyn's parties.

Living It Up- Ann Jennings

When he walked in there were people all over carrying trays of empty glasses, he heard a humming noise, he heard a vacuum running upstairs, two men were washing the windows, a lady was coming down the stairs with an arm full of sheets, when he looked into the living room a man with a big machine was cleaning the couch trying to get a stain out, that was the humming noise he heard when he came in.

The pictures on the walls were all crooked and he noticed the expensive curtains he had made were ripped. He went upstairs to find Carolyn still in bed sleeping with her eye pads on and earplugs in, he called her name twice but she couldn't hear him so he raised the eye pads from her eyes and she opened her eyes looking at him. Oh how was the funeral she asked, we need to talk Lawrence said. Five weeks later Carolyn was on her way back to back to her one bedroom apartment, Lawrence had had enough, and she was no help to him in none of his businesses or his campaign for governor.

Living It Up- Ann Jennings

Two years later Lawrence and Myra Jean were planning a wedding; Myra had heard of Lawrence reputation in the past and had to put her trust in him because it would be a significant aspect that would affect her whole life. The flowers were exquisite, all the shapes, sizes, and every color in the rainbow. The hors d'oeuvres were flown in from Italy, Lawrence loved Italian food. He had a friend from Italy who would come and prepare the food at the mansion. Pete and Lawrence had been friends for years. Pete owned Capellini's on Fifth Street. He was friends to Lawrence and Carolyn and hosted a few of Carolyn's parties.

Now Lawrence was marrying Myra Jean fourteen years his junior. Carolyn and Lawrence never agreed on anything the whole time they lived together accept at the end when they agreed that they made a mistake by living together. After Carolyn moved out the mansion, Lawrence hired Myra Jean from an interior decoration service to redo the entire mansion.

Myra Jean and her group was there every day measuring, matching colors, changing light fixtures, replacing some of the wood doors with glass bringing in more light to each room, all accept the eight bed rooms after six months there were no signs of Carolyn in the entire mansion. On the final day Myra Jean sent the others home telling them she would see them tomorrow at the office.

She waited for Lawrence with the keys and a final bill to his newly remolded mansion. She walked the halls one last time looking in every room admiring her work. When she finished her tour she came back down stairs to find the man of the house standing there in awe. You like Myra Jean asked?

I love it Lawrence managed to say you did just what I wanted you to do; I see no signs of Carolyn anywhere. You even took away that ugly black and gold vase that sat on the shelf by the front door he said "I hated that vase." That's beautiful Lawrence said pointing to the built in shelves on the wall leading to the dining room with beautiful peach sculptures two shades darker than the peach walls. Would you like a tour Myra Jean asked him watching his eyes taking in all her hard work?

Living It Up- Ann Jennings

After dinner he said, are you asking me out to dinner? Yes Lawrence said I think you deserved it, what's your favorite food? Um, well I don't know Myra Jean said stumbling with her words you like Italian Lawrence said. Sure Myra Jean said, well Italian it is Lawrence said guiding her out the front door. You might want to see my bill first Myra Jean said handing him the envelope, I can go over it with you at dinner Myra Jean said, Lawrence took the envelope from her and put it in his briefcase saying I don't deal with such boring details I trust you now Ms. Brooks shall we go? Lawrence opened the door on the Mercedes for Myra Jean she had never felt such comfort in a car, and the leather seats was so soft she sank into them.

They passed her Ford truck in the drive way and went left toward Capellini's on fifth street. Over dinner Myra Jean tried to talk business to Lawrence but he kept changing the subject back to her. He wanted to know everything about her. And by the end of the dinner he knew everything he needed to know. When he introduced Pete to Myra Jean Pete winked at him showing his approval. On the ride back Lawrence invited Myra Jean out the next evening, I just built you a beautiful kitchen don't you want to eat in your own kitchen.

Ok Lawrence said you got the keys, and you know what time I get home. The refrigerator and the pantry is stocked, and the wine cellar is also stocked. Then Lawrence thought "you can cook can't you?" You'll see tomorrow Mr. Middleton you just come home with an appetite. When they returned to Lawrence house he told her I'll take that tour now. As they walked the halls Myra Jean asked him why him and Carolyn never got married she didn't want to Lawrence said and she never wanted kids. So why buy such a big house Myra Jean asked?

Living It Up- Ann Jennings

Carolyn liked to give dinner parties, she was known for her lavish parties, and people would come from Italy and Paris. I gave her an unlimited charge card and let her have her fun because it made her happy. People would come and drink our fine wines, eat our expensive foods, sleep in our guest suites get up and go home and wait for her to invite them again which she did. As fast as she could get a cleaning crew in here she was planning her next party. There were people always walking around and sleeping in our house, I just paid the bill. After almost a year I had enough and said no more she said she couldn't disappoint her friends like that they all looked forward to her parties. That was our last argument before the break up. So is she still having the parties Myra Jean asked yes but not as elaborate Lawrence said and not at my expense.

After the tour Lawrence was very impressed with everything and he told Myra Jean so as he walked her to her truck and asked her why she wasn't married. According to statistic's they don't work Myra Jean shot back. Lawrence stood there with his mouth open to say something but for the first time in his life at a loss for words. He held the door open on her truck for her and said goodnight. The next day at 3:00 Myra Jean arrived at Lawrence house, she knew he liked Italian food so she prepared the only Italian dish she knew, homemade ravioli stuffed with mushrooms and veal with a white sauce.

She found everything she needed in the freezer and pantry, except for the rolling pin. She rolled the doe as flat as she could with her fingers. She found a fancy table cloth and candles in the hall closet. When Lawrence walked into his house it brought back memories of Carolyn's parties. The aroma made his mouth water but only this time he knew he wasn't out of thousands of dollars. Myra Jean was lighting the candles on the kitchen table when he walked into the kitchen. Are we eating in here Lawrence asked? The dining room is to big Myra said. I've never eaten in here before Lawrence told her.

Living It Up- Ann Jennings

Myra Jean dropped the stuffed ravioli one at a time into the bubbly white sauce cooking on the stove. That smells wonderful Lawrence said peeping into the pot. She put butter on the Italian bread and put it on the grill in the middle of the stove. Shall I pour the wine Lawrence said? Yes the glasses are chilling in the freezer Myra Jean told him, just to let you know it's best to drink wine at room tempter Lawrence told her, well thanks for the information, I think I'll be learning a lot about wine from you. Just stick with me kid I'll teach you the ropes Lawrence said laughing and Myra Jean threw the dish towel she was holding at him.

Lawrence had never had stuffed ravioli before but it sure smelled good and he couldn't wait to taste it. Lawrence had always thought ravioli was for kids but they were actually pretty good, and the salad and bread was good also alone with the chilled wine. How many times do we have to date before I ask you to marry me Lawrence said while putting a fork full of salad into his mouth? You don't even know me Myra Jean said; I thought that's what we were doing getting to know each other Lawrence said. Ask me anything you want Lawrence said.

Living It Up- Ann Jennings

What's your middle name Myra Jean asked?
Are your parents still living Myra Jean asked?
We just buried my mother about three months
ago and her mom eight months before her. I
graduated from college and got rich, I have
four brothers; my oldest brother passed away,
my father, grandmother and my youngest
brother lives in Chicago. I'm a triplet, the
youngest of us three was born with oxygen
deficient and even though we're the same age
he functions at the age of a teenager, Myra
Jean notice tears in Lawrence eyes as he
talked about his brother. I never wanted to be
around him when we were coming up, I was
always embarrassed of him but now I know it's
not his fault he was born the way he is.

We have two older brothers and my mom has two older brothers and they are successful in their business. What about you Lawrence said, not so fast Mr. Middleton, I have more questions. Fire away Lawrence said leaning back in his chair laughing. How old are you? How long have you been in politics? Was your dad in politics? When's your birthday? "Woo Woo" you're going to fast Lawrence said my dad is retiring next month and my birthday is August 17th. Well I think I've asked enough questions for one day Myra Jean said but I'll have more questions the next time. "What I don't get a turn Lawrence asked?" next time Myra Jean said. Do you stay close Lawrence asked?

Are you kidding I can't afford to stay anywhere near here. I manage an interior decorating company and my studio apartment is the size of your master suite. Would you like to have a family one day or do you already have one he asked? No it's just me she said. My parents live in their Detroit house in the summer and in their Jacksonville Florida home in the winter, they do this every year. My mom is a retired judge and my dad owns a line of hardware stores in Florida and Detroit. Do you think they would stay in one spot long enough for me to ask for your hand in marriage? I think they would say it's too soon.

We have seen each other and communicated for six months Lawrence said that's a long time. And I would like more of these delicious dinners. "Oh" you want a cook do you? After that dinner there were many more, Lawrence learned Myra Jean Taylor came from Detroit Michigan the only child of Charles and Pamela Taylor. She landed a job at a big interior decorating company in Miami and got her own apartment and worked her way up to management. The job they done for Lawrence was their biggest job ever, the owner told her that it would be too much for them to handle but Myra Jean told her she wanted to try.

He found out her birthday was on New Year's Day four years before his. After two years of dating Myra Jean was planning her marriage to Lawrence. He left all the planning up to her and told her the sky's the limit and she was in complete control. Pam came down from Detroit to help her daughter plan. Lawrence fell in love with his future in-laws. He and Charles had a lot in common, Lawrence asked Pete to be his best man and Pete was happy to do it. Myra Jean and her mom flew to Paris to buy the dress. Myra Jean asked her boss to stand up with her; she was the first person Myra Jean meet when she moved to Miami and offered her a job. All the other girls got jealous so Myra Jean had them all to stand with her.

The wedding was set for January 1st on her birthday Lawrence called his dad and brothers. His dad said if Mickey was feeling ok he would come because he was getting too much for his mom to handle. Eugene and Ronald his two older brothers said they would come, and Richard said Paris was pregnant again and he didn't want to leave her. Carolyn read about the wedding and called to congratulate Lawrence. Lindsey Renee also read about the wedding and called her friend Helen crying. The wedding turned out to be the talk of the town; it made the news and the New York Post. For a wedding gift Pete gave them all five of his cook books, and Myra Jean's boss turned the interior company over to her saying she was moving to St. Thomas and opening up another shop there.

Living It Up- Ann Jennings

Lawrence left a reliable person to run his company while he and Myra Jean was on their honeymoon in Sydney Austria, Myra Jean's boss said she would stay until they returned in three weeks. The three weeks in Australia was the best three weeks of Myra Jean's life. They ate at a different restaurant every day, they went on tours and shopping sprees, Lawrence enjoyed seeing his wife having so much fun. When they returned to the States Myra Jean went to pack her things in the studio apartment. One week later her boss moved and she was in charge of the Florida shop, she promised all the girls that everything would stay the same because everyone in the shop got along well.

Myra Jean started using the new cook books Pete have gave them surprising Lawrence every night with a different dish. The happy couple was invited to lots of parties, and Lawrence made lots of promises to the people turning the party into a campaign, they even got an invitation to one of Carolyn's parties, most of the invitations they had to turn down.

Living It Up- Ann Jennings

At the end of March Lawrence had to rush Myra Jean to the emergency room and they said she had, had a miscarriage which came as a surprise to them because they didn't know Myra Jean was pregnant. She stayed in bed for a week, then in May she had a second miscarriage, this time she stayed in bed for a month. Her mom came down to take care of her. You can always adopt you know she told her daughter, and Pete suggest they go see a specialist.

After many test and thousands of dollars Myra Jean told Lawrence she gives up, it just wasn't meant to be. The end of December Lawrence took Myra Jean to Italy for her birthday the vacation was very romantic. Then in February Myra Jean went to the doctor only to find out she was two months pregnant, the other pregnancies' lasted three and a half months so Myra Jean was expecting to lose this one too. As the months passed Myra Jean's stomach started stretching and she started sleeping more. When she went to the doctor she didn't have her hopes up. When he examined her he asked her would she like to see the babies. Babies Myra Jean said? Look at the screen her doctor said it looks like twins. Myra Jean looked at the screen seeing two images moving around inside her.

Do you hear that sound the doctor said that's the baby's heart beating, Myra Jean started to cry. Are they ok, will they live she asked, everything looks fine and the babies look healthy. Would you like to know the sex of the babies he doctor asked her, yes please Myra Jean said behind her tears. The doctor took a closer look at the screen and said they are two healthy boys. Myra Jean rushed home and fixed Lawrence the best Italian dinner ever, she had to call Pete to ask him a question about one part of the recipes that she didn't understand.

Then she waited with a big smile on her face rubbing her stomach. She called her parents; she had to tell someone, they were so happy for them. When Lawrence came home that evening he opened the door to the best aroma he ever smelled. The table was set and a bottle of champagne was chilling in the ice bucket, fresh flowers were on the table and Myra was humming in the kitchen. When she heard her husband come in she came to meet him wearing a sexy rap dress.

Living It Up- Ann Jennings

Wow Lawrence said are we celebrating? Sit down papa, Papa? Lawrence said are you serious he said while sitting heavily in the chair. Yes I am and not just one but twins, Twins? Lawrence asked are you sure? I've seen them both on the monitor at the doctor's office and heard their heart beats. They held each other and cried until they smelled a burning smell coming from the kitchen, oh no Myra Jean said when they went into the kitchen it was full of smoke.

They both laughed, well there goes dinner. How about we skip dinner and go straight to desert Lawrence said while picking his wife up and carrying her up stairs. After making love Lawrence fell asleep with his ear on Myra Jean's stomach listening. At 2: am they both woke up starving. Myra Jean cracked the eggs while Lawrence graded the cheese. They sat at the kitchen table eating their eggs and talking about the babies. We should pick names Myra Jean said, How about Lawrence after me and Charles after your dad Lawrence said ok that's it Myra said it's settled the first one born will be Lawrence and the second one will be Charles.

Living It Up- Ann Jennings

Now we can talk to them by name Myra Jean said. Lawrence came around the table to rub his wife's stomach, hi Lawrence, hi Charles then he felt a series of kicks. I think they heard me he said getting excited. That would be Lawrence he gives the orders Myra Jean said, how do you know Lawrence asked? He's the one down low, he moves a lot, and Charles is the one up here Myra Jean said placing her hand at the top of her stomach. He don't move as much as his brother, it's like Lawrence would kick for one or two minutes and then he would tell Charles it's ok to kick and he would kick one time. That's my boy Lawrence said sticking his chest out.

Have you told anyone else Lawrence asked? Just my parents Myra Jean said I couldn't wait. We should call everybody Lawrence said, it's three in the morning Myra Jean said I don't think they would appreciate us calling this early in the morning. Not now Lawrence said I mean when the sun comes up. The next morning the first person Lawrence called was his friend Pete, and then he called his dad and brothers. Richard told him Paris was also pregnant with number six and they should get together and celebrate. I don't think I can get any time off right now Lawrence said I just took three weeks off and I really need to get my campaign going again.

Living It Up- Ann Jennings

After Lawrence hung up Myra Jean told him she would love to go to Georgia and visit Richard and Paris. Three weeks later Lawrence put her on a plane and sent her north. Paris picked her up at Hearts field Jackson International Airport in Atlanta.

The two girls went to lunch in Bulkhead and ate out on the terrace and caught up on all the news. I would love to see the hotel Myra Jean told her, after lunch Paris took her and gave her a tour of the Middleton then the sister in-law's got a massage and got their nails done. Paris took her up and introduced her to her mom. When they went to Paris and Richards's house the boys were excite to see their aunt.

When Richard came home from work he and the boys treated the women by cooking dinner. Myra Jean stayed for a week and when she called Maria to tell her she would be returning the next day Maria told her everything was ok at the shop and for her to just enjoy herself. Lawrence put in fifteen hour days all that week while his wife was away he had his staff to find out all the dirt on his component Mattie Hunter that they could find but when they came back with the report it wasn't what Lawrence had wanted to hear.

Mattie Hunter graduated top in her class and was voted to be the most likely to succeed and then went on to college where she graduated as valedictorian in her class, and made the dean's list Lawrence was not happy with their findings and said he would think of something.

When Myra returned home Lawrence went back to regular time. The news media found out about the babies and it was in the paper the next day. Did you tell them Myra Jean asked? No they have their own way of finding out things Lawrence said. Three days after her visit with Paris Myra Jean caught the flu from Benjamin who caught it from a kid at school. She had to stay in bed and let it take its course.

The sound of the phone startled her she hadn't slept in three weeks in her flue like state. It was very rarely that she slept at all but for some reason she guess it was the rain that was helping her sleep this night. She looked at the clock and it was 3:02 a.m. who would be calling her at 3:00 in the morning she thought. She answered the phone in her sleepy voice letting the caller know they just woke her out of a good sleep.

As she brought the receiver closer to her ear she could hear her father in law crying and wondered what it could be. Hi dad what's wrong Myra Jean asked? Hi Myra may I speak to Lawrence Thomas said. She woke Lawrence and told him it was an emergency. She handed him the phone and just sat back and listened to what he was saying on their end. After about thirty seconds Lawrence began to cry Myra Jean's father in law was laconic when he talked to her on the phone but extremely talkative on the phone with his son.

The paramedics and police had just come down from Mickey's room and the police officer, McCoy had to give Thomas the bad news. I'll call Richard Lawrence told his dad. After hanging up Lawrence told Myra his brother Mickey had passed away, his grandmother went in his room to check on him like she did every night but this time Mickey was having hard time breathing so she called to her son to call 911. When the police and paramedics arrived they tried to save Mickey but with no luck. He told her his father was a total wreck ever since officer McCoy and the paramedics arrived at midnight.

"Midnight" Myra said? Why did it take them so long to call us? Because Dad couldn't remember our number that he knew by heart when he went to bed last night. Myra Jean said you should call Richard and Paris, I know you two are not close but this is for Mickey. Will you pack me a bag Lawrence asked her? "I'm going too" No you're not I'm calling your parents to come stay with you. You know how fussy my mom is; she won't let me do anything, not even walk to the mailbox to get the mail. Lawrence reminded Myra of her big shipment of material coming in from Italy in two days, oh yes I forgot about that she said.

After Lawrence made the dreadful call to his brother he told Thomas he would drive to Georgia and they could drive to Chicago together. After hanging up from his brother him and Myra Jean laid in each other's arms and cried. At five A.M. Lawrence was on 95 on his way to Georgia. When he reached Georgia at five P.M. he was exhausted. Paris asked was Myra Jean in the car? No Lawrence said she's sick and she also has a busy week coming up. Paris was not able to go with them she had turned out to be a big time lawyer that everyone counted on. She was always busy if not at work she was on the phone belling out orders and she had a case in three days and a man's life was on the line.

Living It Up- Ann Jennings

They decided that they would take Lawrence car to Chicago. Richard put his suitcase in Lawrence trunk and said he would drive first for the twelve hour drive. Lawrence told her that Myra Jean would call and check on her, and that her parents are on the way to Florida, Paris told him that's good she shouldn't be alone. When the car was all packed Paris kissed her husband and told him to drive safely, something she told him every time he walked out the door. Thomas called his best friend to tell him about Mickey.

Dominique came right over, when will it ever end Dominique asked. He really liked Mickey; he would come by and take him to the gas station that he managed. Mickey liked helping out, wiping down the counters, straighten the soda bottles in the cooler, but his favorite was stocking the candy aisle because he knew Dominique would give him one when he finished. He never talked about his oldest brother DJ when he was with Dominique. Dominique didn't think he remembered him. He called him uncle D and not putting two and two together and knowing he was DJ's father.

Living It Up- Ann Jennings

Thomas liked the time his youngest son spent with his best friend it gave Sheeree free time to do what she wanted. When Mickey was home she had to give him all her attention. He was very busy and always wanted to touch things. They had to keep him out the refrigerator and pantry because he had a lot of allergies. When he went to work with Dominique he knew not to put anything in his mouth unless Dominique gave it to him and he couldn't touch the vitamins because he was allergic to them too. Before they found this out Dominique had him putting the bottles of vitamins on the shelf and Mickey started coughing out of control and sweating profusely.

Dominique snatched him up, put him in the truck and took him to the Doctor's office down the street. When he arrived at the Doctors office he called Thomas and he rushed there with Mickey's medical card. When he arrived the doctor had already given Mickey an allergy shot to stop the coughing and sweating. Thomas asked Dominique what Mickey had eaten. Dominique told him they had not had lunch yet, did he touch anything the doctor said he was stocking the vitamins on the shelf when he had the attack Dominique said. I'm going to send you to an allergy specialist to get a skin test the doctor said. Will it hurt Mickey said no Thomas said you had it before and you said your skin looked like waffles remember and you said you liked it when the doctor wrote on your back.

"Oh yea" I remember Mickey said, it didn't hurt, that's my boy Thomas said. So would you like to take the rest of the day off Dominique asked Mickey, yes sir Mickey said, but can I come in tomorrow? It's up to your dad Dominique said. I'll have him ready in the morning Thomas said. I can show Tracy my back Mickey said. Thomas gave Dominique a look; she's the one I told you about that come in with her mom every day for cappuccino. And when Mickey's not here she asked about him.

Tracy's my girlfriend Mickey said, both Thomas and Dominique laughed. Dominique said well I have to get back. Just how many hours are you putting in there Thomas asked, nineteen hours a day Dominique said that's too many hours; well I'm just sitting in my office doing paperwork; I know you're putting in long hours yourself Dominique said, yes but I'm about ready to give it up. Since Tori left it's no fun anymore, she brought life to the company. I miss her a lot, she was my first love, mine too Dominique said, they both laughed.

Jan called to tell Thomas she would be arriving the morning of the funeral and had to leave that night. After the two brothers left Florida Myra put the coffee pot on and waited for her parents to arrive. When Charles and Pam arrived they started throwing out orders just like Myra Jean had predicted. She went to get the broom and sweep the kitchen floor and her father took the broom from her and told her to go sit down. They wouldn't even let her open the dishwasher to put her coffee cup in. When the phone rang Pam told Myra Jean you just relax I'll answer the phone, and when she found out it was from work she told her daughter she should take a few days off. I can't mom Myra Jean said I have a big shipment coming in.

Living It Up- Ann Jennings

When Paris called later that night the two sisters in laws talked about Mickey, he was so sweet Paris said and my kids adored him. Myra Jean could hear the boys in the back ground, the boys are still crying over the news. Richard and Lawrence drove in silence for the first two hours. Do you need a break Lawrence asked his brother, maybe just to have a cup of coffee Richard said; They stopped and bought coffee and Lawrence took over the drive for two hours and they stopped to eat then Richard took over again, by that time they were high in the mountains it had started to rain the rumble of the thunder was heard in the distance and the wind sounded like a storm was coming and then a string of light shot across the sky.

I would like for us to start over again and become friends and brothers Lawrence said. It's a little too late for that brother, Richard said. So what are you saying Lawrence asked? "Oh would you like for me to start from the beginning" From as far back as I can remember you have been trying to live your life and mine too and making mine a living hell and you want to be friends? Sure you gave me advice and favors but they were all in your favor, to your own advantage you even went and put them in the paper, "Governor gives advice to brother."

Living It Up- Ann Jennings

You do me one favor and you never let me live that down, you keep bringing it up every time someone's around who you would like to impress. I don't even know why you're going to this funeral, you never liked our brother, Richard said crying, and you were going to let him pull a pot of boiling water down on his head. You make everyone look bad around you as long as you look good. I've changed Lawrence said. You never said one word to him, you covered your ears when he cried, you never wanted to dress like us, when our grandmother dressed us you would spill something on your cloths just to put on something different, when I would ask you to play with me and Mickey you would say "you play with him."

 You disgust me and I'm ashamed to call you my brother. Then you go and run for Governor, you couldn't have picked a better job, it fit's you, full of lies and empty promises. After two hours of Richard's telling his brother how he felt the rain was getting heavy but he didn't want to pull over he just wanted to get to Chicago and see his dad.

Living It Up- Ann Jennings

Lawrence apologized for all the wrong doings he had done and told his brother how sorry he was and to please give him another chance to make things right between them. It's a lot to forget Richard said I hope my boys don't grow up to be like you. Me too Lawrence said with his head down, do you mind if I close my eyes for a little while and then I will take over the wheel Lawrence said? Go right ahead Richard said.

After resting for an hour and a half Lawrence woke and asked Richard was he ok. I'm ok I just need to see dad and grandma I know they're a nervous wreck, I know I should have flown, I'm sorry Lawrence said I just thought if we drove together that would give us time to bond. Lawrence yarned and said I'm going to close my eyes for another thirty minutes, if you need me I'm right here and before Lawrence could close his eyes all the way Richard turned the corner on the mountain and a big truck was heading toward them out of control coming from the opposite direction, Richard lost control of the car and slammed into the side of the mountain.

When the call came into the 1st district Police Station Officer McCoy was on his way out after working the midnight shift and heard the officer at the desk on the phone. An out of control car hit the side of the Tennessee Mountain killing two people inside. The two deceased were identified as Lawrence and Richard Middleton and according to the last numbers in each ones phone they went to a Thomas Middleton of Chicago in the first district, and they needed an officer to deliver the news. Hold on Lionel the officer said to officer McCoy I have another job for you. What name did you just say Lionel asked I know that name, what's the address? Hold on I'll look it up another officer at the desk said.

Then the officer came back with Thomas address officer McCoy said that poor man, I'm on my way this is one part of the job that you never get used to. Where are they taking the bodies he asked? The officer was still on the phone with the Tennessee police department and he told them the bodies will be transported to Mercy hospital on Fifth Street. The dispatch had done their part, the station had done their part and now it was McCoy's turn to do his part. Family notifications were the hardest part of his job. On the way to Mr. Middleton's house for the second time Lionel McCoy thought to himself how could a man lose all three of his youngest sons in three days?

Living It Up- Ann Jennings

This was the time he was glad Wanda and him didn't have any kids, they had tried for years until the doctor told her that she could not conceive; even though their house was still always full of kids every day when Lionel came home, Wanda's sister would be there with her kids looking for a bite to eat, and once they were all full they would tell them that they would see them tomorrow. Wanda enjoyed the kids and her sister over every day so Lionel kelp his mouth shut. Lionel sat in his squad car in front of the Middleton house for a couple of minutes before getting out.

When Thomas opened the door and saw Lionel a worried look came to his face. May I come in Lionel asked, sure Thomas said thinking he had come back to check on them. After he gave Thomas the news of Lawrence and Richard Thomas fell to the floor screaming and officer McCoy called for an ambulance. When Sheeree Middleton heard her son crying she came into the living room and found officer McCoy holding Thomas as he cried. Sheeree asked what was wrong and Thomas tried to tell her but couldn't get the words out so Lionel had to tell her and she broke down like her son.

Then he heard the sounds of the sirens and went to open the door. After he explained the situation to the paramedics they found Thomas on the couch crying and Sheeree in the chair crying uncontrollable. They both had to have a shot to calm down Sheeree had not stopped crying since Mickey passed, she had been in his life for over thirty years, it was something special about Mickey, since he came home from the hospital Sheeree held him constantly. She told Tori any time she needed a baby sitter to give her a call, now the grandson that she loved so much was gone.

They were all born together and now they will be buried together. The news of the accident was all over the news and paper the next morning, the station got over one hundred calls before seven that morning people wanting to know the names of the deceased because the news did not give the names yet. They only said two brothers died when their car hit the side of the Tennessee Mountain early Saturday morning. The family was notified of the accident and the names will be released to the public on the 12:00 news.

Living It Up- Ann Jennings

When Jan heard the news she was at work eating a sandwich on her lunch break. She put her head in her hands and started to cry. She called Rose to tell her Dominique's brothers had died in an accident early this morning in the Tennessee Mountains. I heard about that on the news Rose said, they were Dominique's brothers? Yes Jan said "oh I'm so sorry" Rose said where are you? I'm at work Jan said, would you like for me to come to Chicago Jan said not today Jan said buy I would like for you to attend to the funeral with me, anything Rose said.

When Rose got home that evening form work her mom was sitting in front of the TV crying, the news saying two brothers were killed while traveling to another brothers funeral. Her mom had been crying all day for the boy's she didn't even know Rose held her mom and they cried together. I knew their brother Rose told her mom and I'm going to the funeral, I'll go with you her mom said I just feel so sorry for that mother and father.

Marvaleen called Jan when the names were released to see if she had heard the news. "Oh honey I'm so sorry to hear about Dominique's brother's" how could this happen Jan cried into the phone I want to call their dad but I don't know what to say to him. Why don't you leave work early and go home and JJ and I will meet you there in forty five minutes. Thomas had Lawrence and Richard's body's flown to Chicago to be buried in the family cemetery. Sheeree Middleton tried to be strong for her son but what he didn't know was she cried herself to sleep every night. Five days later was the funeral, people came in from all over the world, and the funeral was packed. Rose and her mom drove in from Wisconsin to be with Jan.

Living It Up- Ann Jennings

Marvaleen and Jesus left the baby with her parents to attend the funeral. Sergeant Lionel McCoy came to show his support to the family. Jan, Marvaleen and Jesus sat together. Marvaleen put her arm around Jan every time she started to cry. Jan didn't get a chance to see Rose because it was so many people there. The ushers started ushering parishioner's around to view the body's for the last time Jesus and Marv held on to Jan as they walked around. Jan kissed Thomas and his mom, Ronald and Eugene Dominique's two older brothers on the front pew and told them how sorry she was, she shook hands with Paris and Myra knowing they must be the wives, and they both looked pregnant. London sat behind Paris with the boy's and Ronald and Kenny sat behind their brother in law.

Shirley sat directly behind Kenny for support when he needed her. Leigh Kay hugged Thomas and cried uncontrollable. Lindsey Renee flew in to say goodbye to a man she thought she could have but had no luck, and so did Carolyn. John Miller came but couldn't make himself go up to see his friend in the casket. Pete Luciano just stood there frozen looking at his friend in one of the three caskets. They had all three boy's dressed alike, dark suit's white shirts and red tie's. Pete stood there so long holding up the line Myra got up from her seat and went to him and put her arm around him and they both stood there and cried together looking at her husband and his friend.

When finally they moved away Mattie Hunter and the Mayor of Miami alone with Lawrence staff was next in line to view the bodies. They shook everyone's hand on the first and second row and gave their condolences. Everyone from Capable Hands Insurance Company was there to give their support also. Next in line was Rose and her mom Rose Ann, after they viewed the bodies they walked to the front roll to give their condolences Rose Ann was blowing her nose and wiping her tears away then she saw him, it had been over thirty years but she still remembered. She hugged him and told him how sorry she was.

After the funeral and burial they all went to the hall that was rented for the wake. It was so packed but Rose Ann had to talk to Thomas to see if he remembered her. When she finally found him he was sitting at the table with his mom, two sons and two other men whom she found out later was his brother in laws. You don't remember me do you Rose Ann asked I'm sorry I've seen so many people in the last week but you look very familiar Thomas said someone from my past. How about over thirty years ago on my way to college at the gas station in Georgia "oh my gosh 'Rose Ann' right?"

Thomas stood and gave her a hug. Mom this is the girl I was talking about at the gas station when you took me to Florida to start college. What are you doing here Thomas asked I'm here with my daughter who is a friend of Jan's. You still live in Wisconsin Thomas asked, yes still there Rose Ann said when they looked up everyone had left the table and they were alone talking. I never forgot you Thomas told Rose Ann I thought about you a lot, so you say you have a daughter? Yes, Rose Ann said I fell in love at college and got pregnant, dropped out and never talked to him again then two years later when our daughter turned two, I read in the paper that he died on his motor cycle on his way home from school did he even know about his daughter Thomas asked no Rose Ann said.

Living It Up- Ann Jennings

Did you go to his funeral Thomas asked no I didn't go Rose Ann said I guess I should have went and told his parents that they had a granddaughter Thomas told her about his life, starting with Tori, Eugene, Cindy, DJ, Ronald, Eugene and the triplets. Ronald and Eugene greeted the people when they saw their father busy at the table talking to Rose Ann. After talking for two and a half hours Thomas and Rose Ann exchanged phone numbers and said they would talk more the next day. On the way out everyone shook Thomas hand and told him to try to stay strong. Thomas and Sheeree got to bed after two that night his two sons spent the night with their dad and grandma.

For the next three weeks Thomas was busy from the time he got up until very late at night. He made time to call Myra Jean, Paris and his grandsons to check on them. Hanging up his coat one night a piece of paper fell from his pocket and when he picked it up it had Rose Ann's name on it and her phone number he looked at his watch and thought it was too late to call. The next day at work while sitting at his desk and drinking a cup of coffee he thought about Rose Ann again and checked his coat pocket to see if he had the brought the number with him he found the paper in his pocket and dialed the number.

Living It Up- Ann Jennings

The caller ID said Capable Hands Insurance Company and Rose Ann wondered why an insurance company would be calling her. She picked up the phone and said hello, the next voice she heard took her way back. I'm sorry it took me so long to call Thomas told her, why are you calling me from an insurance company Rose Ann said I own the company Thomas said. Would you like to have lunch this weekend Thomas asked her, that would be nice Rose Ann said. I can drive to Wisconsin Saturday Thomas said you pick the restaurant. Rose Ann gave Thomas her address and told him she would see him Saturday at 1:00.

Thomas hadn't smiled in four weeks but found himself smiling when he hung up the phone, his employees noticed it too and when he got home his mom noticed it also. Thomas told her about Rose Ann "oh yes" I remember you were so worried about her that you wanted me to follow her to her first year in college to make sure she got there safely. Saturday morning Thomas woke at five thirty and couldn't just lay there so he got up made his bed, picked out his cloths, showered and was down stairs drinking a cup of tea and watching the early morning news on TV when his mom came down at seven thirty.

Are you excited she asked him? Yes and a little nervous Thomas said. How long does it take to get to Wisconsin his mom asked? One and a half hours Thomas told her. Don't you think you're up a little early she said with a smirk on her face, just a little Thomas said. He left the house at eleven fifteen eager to get there. The ride was pleasant, he had never noticed before how beautiful the trees were. When he got there what he saw was a cute little pink house a little bigger than a little girls play house, pretty flowers were inside the white picket fence the little house looked very homey and comfortable not chic or trendy but solid. Thomas parked his car in the drive way leading to the one car garage and when he approached the porch Rose Ann opened the door.

The aroma came from the house made Thomas mouth water I decided to cook in Rose Ann said it had been a long time since Thomas had a home cooked meal Sheeree spent all her time caring for Mickey when he was alive and never went in the kitchen. The lunch Rose Ann fixed was delicious and Thomas told her so. After they finished eating lunch they sat at the kitchen table talking and Thomas told her about his company. Did you ever marry Thomas asked her? No Rose Ann said I just work and go to the nursing home every Sunday to visit my mom.

Living It Up- Ann Jennings

I love your home Thomas said looking around, he noticed the built in bookshelves in the corner of the living room with very used old books Danielle steel, Mary Higgins Clark, Dean Knootz and Stephan King. My daughter Rose and I love it she said we each have a bed room and we share a bath and kitchen. I love all the colors Thomas said yes each room is a different color Rose Ann said unlike my house that's very dark Thomas said. Before Thomas left they decided to have lunch again the next Saturday the same time. On the drive home Thomas found himself singing to the radio something he hadn't done in years.

After eight months of traveling to Wisconsin every Saturday Thomas asked Rose Ann to marry him. His sons were so happy for him; it's good to see you happy again Eugene told him, I agree Ronald said. Thomas and Rose Ann went to City Hall and had a small ceremony. Rose Ann packed her cloths and moved to Chicago into Thomas house with him and his mom.

Living It Up- Ann Jennings

Rose continued to live in the house in Wisconsin and Rose Ann would come every Sunday to visit her mom in the nursing home and if she misses a Sunday Rose would go for her. Suddenly Thomas kitchen came to life again Rose Ann was cooking three meals every day and one day when Thomas came home Sheeree and Rose Ann was in the front yard planting flowers we can get a gardener for that Thomas said.

We'll take care of the yard his wife said but you can get a painter to paint the inside of the house. Thomas got right on it, the next day the painter showed up while Thomas was at work Sheeree and Rose Ann picked bright colors for each room and when Thomas came home that evening they met him at the door excited and showed him the colors they had picked I love it Thomas said thinking about Rose Ann's house in Wisconsin. Three weeks later the house was bright and the kitchen was always producing aromas out of this world.

Every week end Thomas brought home a briefcase full of work from the office saying he had to work all week end Rose Ann brought him tea and biscotti and rubbed his shoulders what can I do to help she asked him? I could use some help at the office he told her. I can help she told him ok you're hired he told her and started showing her how to fill out insurance forms and documents. They stayed in the din pass dinner time so Sheeree cooked and brought them a tray. The following Monday Thomas took Rose Ann to work and introduced her to the staff he gave her Tori's old office and everyone loved her and unlike their feelings for Tori they welcomed her and told her they could use the help.

The next week end Thomas went out for a beer with Dominique something they hadn't done in years. Well how's it going newlywed? Dominique said, over worked at the office Thomas said anything I can do to help Dominique said? You're good with figures Thomas said how would you like to come and work with me. I wanted to work there over thirty years ago and was turned down Dominique said. Well I own the company now and I'm asking you to come work with me.

How's your mom Thomas asked? She's doing great since she stopped drinking Dominique said. One month later Dominique was working at Capable Hands Insurance Company and two weeks later Thomas offered him and his mom the big house, it's just sitting there empty Thomas told him.

Thomas and Gloria moved into the house in front of Thomas, Rose Ann and Sheeree. Gloria and Sheeree became close friends. Sheeree showed Gloria how to plant flowers which she learned from Rose Ann and Gloria admitted to Sheeree that she had never planted anything before and was thrilled when she looked out her window and saw all the pretty flowers growing in the yard she had planted with her own hands. The two would have coffee in the yard every morning after Thomas, Rose Ann and Dominique went to work.

One week end Thomas and Rose Ann flew to Florida to visit Myra Jean and stayed with her one night and then flew to Georgia to see Paris and the grand kids and stayed one night at the beautiful hotel. He told both his daughter in-law's that they would be back to visit again.

Living It Up- Ann Jennings

When Paris went into labor London and Jackie
was by her side in the delivery room while all
the boys were walking back and forward in the
waiting room. One more push the doctor said
with Jackie on one side and London on the
other Paris gave a big push with all her
strength and the next thing she heard was a
loud wail.

 Tears came to her eyes and all three girls
were crying when the doctor announced it's a
girl. Baby Madison was born weighing eight
pounds and nineteen inches long she's going to
be so tall Jackie said just like her mom London
said. When Paris and Madison was released
from the hospital she called Thomas to tell him
about his new grand daughter and two days
later Thomas and Rose Ann was on the plane
to Georgia leaving Dominique in charge of the
company. They spent three days at the
Middleton Hotel enjoying the grandkids and
Rose Ann took lots of pictures of Madison, she
was the cutest thing she had ever seen with
her little pink face and blond flock.

They returned home with lots of pictures to show Sheeree she told them if they drive down next time she would go with them to see her great grandkids but there was no way she was getting on a plane. Only one month later after they returned from Georgia Myra gave birth to twin girls. Her parents were there for her last month and rushed her to the hospital one morning when she woke up in pain. Myra's mother called Thomas and him and Rose Ann was off again to Florida to see their twin granddaughters. They stayed in Florida for two weeks visiting the twins and then flew back to Georgia for two days to see Madison again.

Promising both Myra Jean and Paris that they would be back to visit and the next time they would drive and bring the kids great grandmother. Mr. and Mrs. Taylor asked Myra Jean to move back home so they could help out with the twins. Myra Jean thought it was a good idea and called Carolyn and asked her if she wanted to buy the house since it was hers from the beginning. One month later Carolyn was moving back into the house she shared with Lawrence so many years ago and Myra Jean and the twins was moving to Jacksonville Florida in the winter with her parents and Detroit in the summer.

Dominique started dating Tracy's mom from the gas station and talking about marriage. Ronald started coming over for Sunday dinner again when his girlfriend was mad at him. Then Eugene started coming too. Three months later Kenny, Shirley and Kevin started coming also. Kenny and Shirley bought a big beautiful house in Indiana just outside of Chicago.

Kenny scheduled his customers to come in on Wednesdays and Fridays, he only went to the shop two days a week now and Glen went in the other three days, and they were closed on Sundays and Mondays. Kenny told Shirley at one Sunday dinner that he loved what she did to the house it had always been white all his life but now each room has color now and he loved all the yellows, lilac, greens, and peach. Hey and by the way what color is my room now Kenny said? Your room Shirley said? You mean the third room on the right up stair's that had the wooden plank "Kenny" on the wall Rose Ann said, that room is now pink and my sewing room.

You have that big house in Indiana you don't need a room here, and that beautiful new Music studio that I read about in the paper. Yes we have been getting a lot of very talented singers coming in Shirley said. I'm going to be a singer Kevin said everyone at the table laughed. This dinner is superb Eugene said. Rose Ann and Sheeree had went way out, everyone had a very large two inch T-bone steak which Thomas cooked on the grill, they also had corn on the cob, baked potato, fresh toss salad, garlic bread, and Sheeree made a peach cobbler. After dinner the men left the dining room and the ladies cleared the table and cleaned the kitchen. When they all got ready to leave they told Thomas and Shirley that they would see them next Sunday.

The End.

Living It Up- Ann Jennings

Living It Up- Ann Jennings

This Book Was Published By Maximize Publishing Inc.

ISBN-13: 978-0692301623
ISBN-10: 0692301623

Maximize Publishing Inc.

(Retail Price 21.99)

www.ingramcontent.com/pod-product-compliance
Lightning Source LLC
Chambersburg PA
CBHW071836020726
47502CB00004B/1382